FOOLED AROUND AND SPELLED IN LOVE

A Cozy Paranormal Mystery

MICHELLE M. PILLOW

Michelle M. Pillow® - MichellePillow.com

The Happily Everlasting Series

COZY PARANORMAL MYSTERY ROMANCE NOVELS

Dead Man Talking

by Jana DeLeon

Once Hunted, Twice Shy

by Mandy M. Roth

Fooled Around and Spelled in Love

by Michelle M. Pillow

Witchful Thinking

by Kristen Painter

Total Eclipse of The Hunt

by Mandy M. Roth

Curses and Cupcakes

by Michelle M. Pillow

An Everlasting Christmas
by Mandy M. Roth

(Un)Lucky Valley - Spin off Series
Better Haunts and Garden Gnomes
Any Witch Way But Goode
More Books Coming Soon

Visit Everlasting
https://welcometoeverlasting.com/

Fooled Around and Spelled in Love

A HAPPILY EVERLASTING SERIES NOVEL

Welcome to Everlasting, Maine, where there's no such thing as normal.

Anna Crawford is well aware her town is filled with supernaturals, but she isn't exactly willing to embrace her paranormal gifts. Her aunt says she's a witch-in-denial. All Anna wants is to live a quiet "normal" life and run her business, Witch's Brew Coffee Shop and Bakery. But everything is about to be turned upside down the moment Jackson Argent walks into her life.

Jackson isn't sure why he agreed to come back to his boyhood home of Everlasting. It's like a spell was cast and he couldn't say no. Covering the Cranberry Festival isn't exactly the hard-hitting news this reporter is used to. But when a local death is ruled an accident, and the police aren't interested in investigating, he takes it upon himself to get to the bottom of the mystery. To do that, he'll need to enlist the help of the beautiful coffee shop owner.

It soon becomes apparent things are not what they seem and more than coffee is brewing in Everlasting.

To my author buddies, and the rest of the Everlasting team: Jana DeLeon, Mandy M. Roth, and Kristen Painter. It's been crazy, magical fun working with you on this project.

Chapter One

WITCH'S BREW COFFEE SHOP AND BAKERY,
EVERLASTING, MAINE

"I don't care if the Massachusetts supplier didn't send Ginger's shipment for the banquet tonight. They're not the only cranberry state in the US. She's just going to have to find new ones or make her super-secret punch from a can." Behind the coffee shop counter, a tall woman of slender build pleaded passionately into her phone. The white apron with the logo of a magical coffee bean covered her distressed denim jeans and fitted V-neck t-shirt. It was still clean, as if she had yet to actually bake anything that day. "The festival is starting tomorrow and I need my cranberries, or these orders won't be filled."

She lifted a giant stack of papers and shook them as if the person she talked to on the phone could hear how many there were. Something about the way she spoke said she knew the person on the other end of the line well. Her wavy dark hair was wound into a messy bun at the nape of her neck that threatened to uncoil.

Her expression was both desperate and frustrated, giving the impression she had a whole host of things hanging by a thin thread. "Now, I need you to get back in your truck, and then drive straight to my shop with my cranberries. You know how busy this month is, and I'm already behind schedule."

Jackson Argent watched the agitated woman carefully, glad that she had no clue he was there. He'd projected his consciousness into the coffee shop to peek inside before it opened for business. To her he'd be as see-through as air. People revealed so much when they thought no one was looking.

Surely this couldn't be the same Anna Crawford that he'd been told to hire as a photographer. She looked beyond busy running the Witch's Brew Coffee Shop and Bakery. There was a chaotic grace to the way she moved as if her thoughts pulled in fifty different directions, but she never let one of those metaphorical balls drop. She didn't try to hide the frustration in her lovely dark eyes. His breath caught a little as he watched her. Man-oh-man, she was beautiful.

The small business had the familiar, homey feel of most locally owned coffee shops. Specialty mugs with the magical bean logo perched in the corners of the room, a constant reminder of where you were. It was smart advertising. The mismatched chairs, and heirloom tables instantly put you at ease and welcomed customers to hang out awhile. Painted concrete floors added an industrial appeal while being easy to keep clean. In the center of the cozy place were large comfortable couches that faced each other for meaningful conversation. Overlooking them were exposed wooden beams with beautiful patterns in the grains. Photographs of the town and its people hung on the coarse brick walls.

The pictures were unusual, taken from interesting angles—wrinkled faces and old buildings with ancient facades, a woman riding an adult tricycle with a cat, torn pieces of paper that curled perfectly. There was one of two men, young and rough, caught deep in animated conversation on a wharf near the old lighthouse.

Seeing her work, Jackson knew he was in the right place. These were not the moments most people snapped pictures of. The photographs on the wall proved that Anna Crawford saw what most people missed.

Jackson approached the counter slowly and glanced at the woman's name tag. "Anna." Yep, it was her.

"Don't Anna-sweetheart me, George," Anna warned. "If you're not here in ten minutes, you can explain to the fifty-billion PTO members why their kids don't have their good luck cranberry cookies in their lunch boxes next Wednesday. Then you can explain to the hospital why they don't have cranberry muffins. Then you can tell Sheriff Bull and her calendar boys why they don't have cranberry scones. And you can be sure that I'll let everyone know at the banquet tonight—*including your mother*—why the Sacred Order of Hairy Old Men's cranberry kickoff is—" She set the stack of orders down in irritation. "I know there are not literally fifty-billion people in the PTO."

Anna leaned on the counter, propping her head as George presumably responded. Her eyes moved over a display near the register as if silently studying the tea boxes, candles, local pottery, and bottles of coffee flavoring that were for sale. There was something about this woman that reminded him of his ex-girlfriend, Nicole Phillips. Nicole had been a work-a-holic, to the point everything else was more important than their relationship, until she decided she wanted attention. Even though it had been five years, the breakup left him a little jaded when it came to balancing work and life. Sadly, he couldn't blame her as he also worked all the time. Some people weren't meant to be in relationships, so he had thrown himself into his job. It was easy to be bitter about romance.

For a moment Jackson thought of leaving the

coffee shop and taking the photos himself. Anna looked like the type of woman that might complicate his simple life. He had a month after all. It wasn't exactly a hard-hitting assignment covering the so-called mysterious events that seemed to pop up every year during the Everlasting Cranberry Festival. Half of those mysteries would only be printable in a tabloid. The general public wouldn't believe that a troll redecorated and caused earthquakes, or whatever else nonsense happened in the magical village of secret supernaturals. How his editor even found out about this seaside New England town was beyond him.

Great, I have my first story. 'The Mystery of the Missing Cranberries,' he thought sarcastically. *The thing practically writes itself.*

Jackson remembered the town vaguely from when he was a young child, and the feeling of relief he'd felt when his father moved him away from it after his mother's death. Jackson recalled very little about his mother, except the warning she'd whispered to him each night before bed, *"Don't give in to the magic or the hunters will find us. They'll find the town and kill us all."* His mother had not been mentally well. Still, the words had been imprinted on the walls of his mind as a child, and he'd been terrified of Everlasting. As an adult, he wasn't afraid, but he wasn't that eager to be back here either.

Covering a celebration of fruit wasn't exactly

the best use of his investigative skills as a journalist. His editor could have sent him to cover the German Brat and Beer Fest. At least it would feel a little manlier in his portfolio.

Anna took an audible breath and lifted her head. Her dark eyes moved briefly in Jackson's direction, but she didn't see him. "Do better than your best, George. I'm not joking around this time. Get my cranberries back from Ginger."

"Leave poor George alone. I can materialize cranberries with a *bimp* and a *bamp* and a little bit of that," a voice offered from the back kitchen.

When he saw the stressed expression on Anna's face, he felt a little sorry for her. However, when she spoke, she managed to keep her tone even. "Aunt Polly, for the last time, no. I don't need your assistance. You know what happened when I let you in the kitchen to help with the cranberry cookies. They weren't edible."

"I disagree. Those cookies were only a little tainted by the magic of my touch," Polly said. "I do not harm, only help."

"And create chaos," Anna muttered.

"In fact, I was gazing into the crystal ball last night, and I don't want to forget to tell you that you should wear orange on December 20th."

"I'm not doing that," Anna answered.

"Then don't come crying to me when you stub your toe," Polly warned.

Anna grumbled, but he watched her pick up a pocket calendar and write, "Wear Orange," in large print on the aforementioned date.

"How long are you going to hold that one mistake over my head?" Polly asked. "I taught you how to make cookies. You should be glad to have my help in here. They are my recipes you are using after all."

"I took the crazy out of the list of ingredients and replaced it with nutmeg," Anna mumbled, before pleading louder, "Please. Just leave it. George will come through."

"Seriously, when are you going to let me help cook? You need help. You can't do it all, Anna. You take on too much responsibility. Well, you *could* do it all if you used your natural gifts."

"When your garden gnomes come to life and ask me to pick up my witchcraft, I'll listen," Anna whispered sarcastically, before raising her voice so her aunt could again hear her. "How about we ask Hugh Lupine what he thinks? That cake you gave him had him howling at the moon for a week."

"A tiny side effect and I gave him something to treat the fleas afterward." Polly poked her head out of the kitchen. The artificial red of her hair coiled on the top of her head in a bun. It clashed with the lime green of her flour-dusted apron. She wore a navy blue retro dress with a fitted bodice and A-line skirt underneath. Her plastic jewelry was bulky and bright. The plastic frames of her glasses matched the dress. She had a hint of age to her, but the years had obviously been kind. "George hasn't come through for anyone since the second World War."

"That doesn't make sense. He wasn't alive during the World War," Anna argued.

"Reincarnation," Polly said, keeping a straight face. "I was once a princess who was adored by many. I outlived six husbands and two zebras."

"Why is it every person claims to be something special in a past life?" Anna countered.

"Not you," Polly teased, "you were a one-armed peasant with a bad case of the pox and often forgot to bathe."

"Thanks." Anna tried to hide her laugh. "Sweet of you to say. What are you doing in that apron? You promised me that you would behave this year."

"When have I ever promised to behave?" Laughter followed the statement. "I said I wouldn't bake for the Cranberry Festival. I'm making cookies for Principal Bails. You know he's allergic to cran-berries, and I always feel bad for him during this month. The man is taunted with all the delicious foods he can't have."

"I'm sure Sigmund Bails will be fine feeding himself." Anna stepped toward Polly, forcing her aunt backward into the kitchen. "Better than turning into a were-octopus or stuck in wolf form because you decided to sprinkle a little something extra on his cinnamon rolls."

"Don't be silly. Sigmund's bloodline is were-Kraken."

"Polly, where did all these cranberries come from?" Anna demanded from the back. He leaned to the side to try to get a better look, but the small window in the metal door showed him nothing.

"Magic. I grew them out of my ears," Polly teased. Though, in this town, who knew what was possible. "I have many mystical powers."

"*Polly?*" Anna insisted.

"George dropped them off about twenty minutes ago," Polly admitted with a laugh. "He was on the phone with you."

"For the life of me, I don't know why all of you want to give me a heart attack. You know how important this month is. The town explodes with visitors, and it keeps us in business for the rest of the year. It pays our rent and the employees. George should focus on finding his next tourist romance and leave the practical jokes to clowns."

Jackson heard movement in the kitchen. It sounded like crates being pushed around.

'The Mystery of who George will Date,' Jackson mused. He'd give anything for a good political scandal.

"You're not jealous, are you?" Polly asked.

He liked Polly. She seemed like a real character. Maybe he'd find her later and get her talking.

"Of George? Why would I be jealous of who George dates?" Anna scoffed. "Will you stop eating the inventory and help me stock the display case, please?"

"Because everyone in town thinks the two of you should be married." Polly's words were muffled as if she talked with her mouth full.

"Not that again." A crate dropped on the floor, the crash punctuating her words. "You, his mother, and the lady at the bridal shop does not constitute the whole town. You know our relationship was completely misguided."

"So, who's the lurker in the front?" Polly inquired. "He's cute. I like a man who can wear a cashmere sweater."

"What lurker?" Anna asked. "The doors are still locked."

"Mr. Lookie Lou out there watching you in the *murump-enumph…*" Polly's words were lost.

Jackson gasped in shock. Had Polly seen him? How was that even possible? He felt his consciousness pull out of the closed coffee shop, back to where he sat on the bench across the street. He'd arrived early and merely thought he'd take a peek inside Anna's place of work. Secretly screening places before he went inside was an old habit. As a journalist, he needed to use any tools at his disposal to uncover a story. His ability to project part of his soul to other locations came in handy. His father had called it spirit walking. He was able to move through walls and locked doors like a ghost. It was one of the few useful skills his father had given him.

Already, people walked through the historic downtown district, though he could imagine it would become much busier when the festival activities began in full force. Hardworking locals put the finishing touches on the burgeoning event, setting out giant cranberry sculptures and hanging the large banner promising a month-long schedule of activities, music, food, and family fun.

Tourists were easily decipherable from locals. They snapped pictures standing by a large oak tree, by the banners and cranberry decorations. They then set about tagging and posting the selfies on social media.

Clouds churned in the distance as if threatening a storm, but Main Street was spared as bright sunlight warmed the area. Jackson wore a light jacket over his tan sweater and denim jeans. He'd expected the fall day to be cooler than it was, especially being located right next to the ocean.

Across the street, Anna rushed from inside the shop. She scoured the sidewalk and then down the opening of the alley that ran along the side of the café. He imagined she was looking for the invisible intruder in her store. In her flustered state, Anna drew attention of some of the tourists, who naturally gravitated toward the opened door.

As a reflex action, Jackson reached into his jacket for his phone. When Anna glanced across the street at him, he pretended he was checking his messages and was unaware of what was going on.

Chapter Two

"Polly, watch the counter, I'm making a delivery," Anna called as customers lined up to place their orders. She needed fresh air. Polly was in top mischievous form this morning, and it was more than she could handle. Her aunt kept insisting that a handsome, invisible teleporter in expensive cashmere had been inside the store waiting for them to serve coffee.

Anna knew she should have never allowed Polly to sell her magical wares and services out of the back of her shop, but owning her own business made her aunt happy. Plus, customers seemed to like the novelty of Polly's Perfectly Magical Mystical Wondrous World of Wonders, as Polly insisted on naming her store.

Most of the merchandise was harmless—tarot cards, lucky gemstones, spells to help gardens grow

—and others were a little more questionable. Anna had seen love potion bottles and a "secret" list of services that involved several of their family's old magic. The latter came from an ancient grimoire that Anna had been trying to take away from Polly for years. She loved her aunt but questioned her ability to decide who should be cursed, and who should be blessed.

Natural magic on its own was fine, but people were flawed. It was why Anna didn't use her magic. Polly teased her and called her a witch-in-denial. Anna didn't deny her birthright, instead she chose to do things a little more normally, like running her business without magic and making her own deliveries when she could to save money.

Some of the coven witches in town believed curses and spells to be the work of dark magic and had very stringent rules when it came to the craft. They had a right to practice and believe what they wanted, but Polly and Anna didn't necessarily agree with the others' views. Plus, Anna had a strict non-joining policy when it came to clubs and covens. Once in High School, she had been asked to join the Black Hose Society. The girls used their "witch-craft" as an excuse to wear tight skirts and make each other drink weird "potions." There was nothing magical about a bottle of cheap wine cooler mixed with milk and soda—unless the spell was to induce vomiting.

It made sense that the more she could get done before the official start of the festival the smoother the next month would be. Hunted Treasures Antiques & Artifacts Shop received an order of scones each week. Well, more to the point, she always brought over an order of assorted scones and never charged the owner Wilber "Wil" Messing. His son had died nearly twenty years earlier, and his granddaughter, Penelope, had been taken to live with her mother's family. He worked away in his shop as if holding onto the past by collecting antiques.

There was a sadness to the old man to which Anna could relate. She'd lost both her parents at a young age. They'd been touring an old building when the structure gave out and collapsed, killing them both.

The historic building was older than some of the antiques Wil sold, but the green awning over the picture window and front sidewalk were always well-maintained. According to Polly, Wil's family line monitored supernaturals and cursed items. It's why he never let her buy the camera from the "special" section of the store. Truth be told though, it was hard to determine with her aunt just how much of what she said was fiction and how much was fact.

Anna didn't believe in curses. She believed in science—evolution, and genetics. She had certain magical powers because her family line had evolved to have them. It was no different from her having wavy brunette hair and dark brown eyes.

"Mr. Messing?" she called out as she entered the antique shop. Though clean, it was cluttered with antiques of all sizes and shapes. The pieces had been jammed into every available space. He had everything from recovered hardware from old buildings, to architectural fixtures and gargoyles, to iron doors and stained-glass windows. Anna didn't know the significance of half the items, except for the little white tags that gave a description and price. For just under four thousand a customer could be the proud owner of a metal Parisian horse head from 1903. Or for nearly forty thousand, a person could own a 1882 Rosewood Chickering grand piano that had been carved by hand.

Anna bought several of the tables for her coffee shop from him. They weren't worth anything near a four-thousand-dollar horse head, but she liked that they'd been reclaimed from old buildings and repurposed.

"Wil? It's Anna. I have scones. I could use your opinion on the new recipes I'm trying before the full force of the tourist invasion. I have orange-cranberry with vanilla glaze, lemon-cranberry with a lemon glaze, chocolate-caramel-cream cheese with cranberry glaze, cranberry-nutmeg, and a lemon-cranberry-brie concoction that I just thought of last night. Wil? Are you here? I believe that this brie recipe might be ingenious."

There was no response. It wasn't odd for the place to be quiet this time of the morning. The stillness of the shop was soothing. It allowed Anna to gather her thoughts. Mrs. Harmon had mentioned seeing a young woman with Wil. Anna liked to think that it was his granddaughter who had come to visit. The thought made her smile.

Anna made her way toward the front counter. She tripped on a table leg that stuck out. As she stumbled, a bright light flashed, as if she'd somehow triggered a camera strobe. Quickly, she found her footing and then stood. Anna glanced around, looking for clues to what had happened.

"Wil, I'm going to leave them behind the counter for you, all right?" Anna said, tilting her head to listen for any signs of life.

Still, there was no answer.

She sighed.

It was strange that Wil would forget to lock the store when he ran an errand, so chances were he was in the back unpacking a shipment. Anna placed the box on the counter. The smell of fresh baked goods wafted up, making her smile as she arranged the bow on top so it looked pretty before turning to leave.

Another gift caught her eye, this one was wrapped in brown paper and twine. She couldn't help glancing at the card. Her name was printed at the top. She flipped open the card and read the neat cursive script, *"For Anna, I know you've had your eye on this. I haven't been able to sell it to you, for things like this should never be sold, but I must find it a new caretaker as it grows restless to be used. Keep it out of the wrong hands."*

She glanced around, her eyes moving toward the case Wil kept under heavy lock. The items inside it were not for sale. The camera she'd tried to buy from him for the last seven years was no longer in its place.

Anna made a small noise of excitement as she pulled the twine loose and lifted the lid. The sides of the box uniformly collapsed onto the counter. Her hands shook with anticipation as she touched the old, handmade camera. Wil hadn't even let her hold it before.

The polished wood body seemed to pulse with a life of its own, making her fingers tingle. Embossed leather wrapped part of the back, and the brass mounting plate still shone as if it had been recently polished. A small insignia was carved into the base, but she didn't recognize the manufacturer. One thing was for certain—it was definitely older than the early 1900s Brownies already in her collection. If she had to venture a guess, she'd say it dated back to the mid-1800s.

"Wil, I…" Her voice was barely audible. It was the most beautiful piece of camera equipment she'd ever seen. Surely the thing was worth a small fortune. A few thousand at least. "Thank you."

Anna couldn't wait to use her new camera. Excited, she carefully placed it on the counter and wrote a quick thank you note for the gift and slipped it under the bow on the scones. She then fitted the camera into the box to carry it home. That sweet old man would be getting more scones and muffins and cookies than he could eat in a lifetime.

Chapter Three

"Anna Crawford?"

Anna heard the man behind her, but the stranger's words didn't register as she concentrated on the stopwatch app on her phone. As the timer hit one minute, she blocked the light from the lens on the antique camera and smiled at the array of masked men posing for her in the small entry hall of the Diana Lodge banquet hall. They all wore tuxedos with tails, and she'd seen several top hats around. Most of the men had taken their hat off and replaced them with the werewolf masks.

Behind them, the gigantic rock fireplace added a sense of atmosphere to their arrangement. The building looked like a giant hunting cabin on the outskirts of town, the wooden log walls, and old paintings of various big game animals, but no one hunted the nearby woods anymore.

Anna released her held breath. "Thank you, gentlemen. I'll let you know how the photo turns out."

"Did you know the Yao tribe believed that a camera could capture a person's shadow and keep their soul? Imagine how many souls a camera like that has collected," Professor Jonathon Hamilton mused, even though he'd just let her take his picture. He wore a dark gray suit vest with a matching jacket with tails over a white undershirt and thick black tie. The material was shiny and had a modern flair. "I was reading an article about a medical device they were developing in Russia that captured a picture of the soul as it left the body at the moment of death."

"You have nothing to worry about, old chap. You lost your soul to me in a poker game fifteen years ago," Dr. Richard Magnus teased. He was more of an old-fashioned suit man. The material of his jacket seemed to be made of a dark wool blend, and the front panels were cut to waist length. It contrasted the white of his shirt and bow tie.

"Soul stealing cameras? What exactly did you teach, Hamilton? Paranormal pseudo-science?" Order member Douglas Talbot was a retired judge. Like Magnus, he wore an older style suit compared to the others. The main difference was his bow tie was red, not white. Anna had known the judge since she was a child when he'd bring flowers around for Aunt Polly. For some unknown reason he made her uncomfortable now that she was older. Maybe it was because he was actively looking for wife number five.

"I taught biology," Hamilton answered motioning toward a waiter carrying glasses of champagne, "among other things."

The server held a tray for Hamilton to take a flute. He sipped slowly as if contemplating his next move.

"Brandy for me," Magnus ordered.

"If I were to let anyone keep my soul, it would be a Crawford woman," Talbot expressed, with a deep sigh and a hand pressed longingly to his chest. "They do not make them more beautiful than that."

"To the moon, to the stars, to the ocean at night," the order president, Herbert London chanted. By day he was a mediocre real estate agent with a trust fund. He held up his hands to form pretend claws. The unfortunate cut of a tailed tuxedo accentuated the man in all the wrong ways. His rotund physique looked more like a beach ball than a fierce creature of the night.

"*Rawr!*" the gathered men responded in unison.

"To the prey, to the mate, to the first hairy bite," Herbert continued in low tones, inching his way toward Anna.

"*Rawr!*" came the cry.

"To our ancestors who started Everlasting long ago." Herbert placed his hand over his heart.

"To the victor, a prize never to go," Anna dismissed, not wanting to be a part of their evening games. Though powerful men, they were mostly harmless.

However, one year she'd found herself walking back to town after they'd persuaded her to put on the what-turned-out-to-be enchanted rabbit mask. The second she placed it on her head, she took off like prey being chased by hungry wolves. What most people didn't realize was that the Hairy Old Men part of the club name referred to the fact they were founded by shifters.

Luckily, a branch dislodged the thing or else she might have tried to burrow under a tree stump. The men had spent the night drunk in the forest, worried that harm had come to her. She'd managed to find her way home with only a few bruises. Dr. Magnus later confessed they'd all ran into a patch of poison ivy and the cranberries weren't the only red berries that year. It was the last time they wore robes, and the last year anyone touched the rabbit mask.

"You break my heart, miss," Herbert protested with a non-serious pout when she didn't let him finish his werewolf love poem.

"And your wife would break me," Anna laughed. "Hello, Mrs. London."

"Oh, no, you can have him, sweetheart!" Cynthia London, Herbert's wife, offered from the door leading to the banquet hall. The blue, one shoulder, side slit evening gown clung to her as she moved. She looked every bit a hoity-toity woman of high society in her formal wear, stiletto heels, and diamond earrings, but she had a kind heart. Anna had seen her at the animal shelter playing with stray cats. Herbert growled and turned his pretend claws on his wife as he chased her from the room.

"I'm not sure the Sacred Order of Hairy Old Men is quite the right club description," the stranger's voice continued with a small laugh. "I think some of those men haven't grown hair for quite some time."

"Ah, they're a bunch of pussy cats who partook of the cranberry vodka a little early this year. All roar, no bite, maybe a few pranks." Anna glanced at the dispersing crowd as the tuxedoed men pulled off their furry animal headdresses. She then turned to face the man talking to her.

The stranger seemed too young to be a prospective member of the order, and she didn't recognize him as a legacy. Plus, he didn't wear a tuxedo like the others. Short brown hair framed a stunningly handsome face. It wasn't the perfect angular features that made her think that, but a ruggedness that indicated he was a wanderer, unsettled and constantly searching.

A restless energy came from the stranger, a disquiet that could not be restrained by a nice suit. The gray jacket had notched lapels and a two-button closure with only the top button fastened. His hand lifted to finish unbuttoning the jacket to reveal a thin black belt and tailored black slacks. She should not have been looking at his waist and quickly drew her eyes back up to his intense green ones. This was not a man who would have come to Everlasting without reason. She felt that as sure as she felt the air in her lungs.

Her natural magic tried to tingle in her fingers, urging her hand to lift in his direction. She repressed the urge. Anna had constrained her power for so long. She wasn't sure what her magic would do if she let it out.

His expression was overly serious, but his intense eyes looked as if he wanted to smile. Mesmerized by the thoughts swirling from her natural intuition, Anna automatically reached for the nearest camera to take the shot. Unfortunately, the film paper coated in gallo-nitrate of silver needed preparation before she could use the antique. His gaze shifted to the side, and the moment was lost.

Anna glanced down, keenly aware of how underdressed she was compared to all the evening wear. A strand of her wavy hair tickled her cheek. She self-consciously tucked her hair behind her ears and tried to smooth it back into the messy bun. She hadn't seen a mirror since she'd gotten dressed that morning and had taken all of two minutes to get ready for her banquet delivery as she'd slipped into a clean pair of skinny blue jeans and a red three quarter-sleeve t-shirt that wasn't covered in coffee grounds and flour.

"Hey, Anna, thought I'd see you here tonight." George Madison's voice drew her attention away from the stranger. Like the other guests, he wore a black tuxedo with long tails and carried a werewolf half-mask. His clothes looked like he'd found the suit in his great-grandfather's closet, an afterthought to the evening rather than careful planning. "Get your shipment of cranberries?"

"Yeah, I got it," Anna grumbled, feeling the irritation settling in her shoulders, causing the muscles to tense. "You think you're so funny, don't you?"

"Just trying to lighten you up," George teased. "You're always so serious, Anna. You need to learn to smile more. Polly agrees with me."

"If you have to cite Polly as your source of support, you're in trouble. Just this afternoon she tried to tell me her favorite ceramic garden gnome was looking a little sickly." Anna chuckled. "How is your mother? Did Ginger finally receive her cranberries?"

"She's around here somewhere. She wants to know when you're going to come over again for dinner." George's blond hair was tousled messily around his head, and it only added to his boyish charm.

Anna picked up the antique camera and placed

it carefully into the padded red camera bag she'd brought with it.

"What are you doing here, anyway? Don't tell me you're up for membership. I thought one of the requisites of the Hairy Old Men's social circle was to be old." Anna dodged George's dinner invitation. "They'll let anyone into these top-secret clubs, won't they?"

"Captain Tom is dating my mother and trying to impress me by giving me a bid." George grinned. "He knows the way to my mother's heart is through her son's approval."

"And that is won by giving you access to this glorified poker club?" Anna shook her head in mock disappointment.

"Little does Tom know I'm holding out for a new boat," George laughed. "Nothing fancy."

"A ten-million-dollar yacht?" Anna asked.

"Don't be silly. I'd settle for five. There are some nice entry model fly bridge cruisers on the market." George managed to say it with a straight face, but she knew he was joking.

"You still say that like I know what you're talking about." Anna met the gaze of a woman standing against the wall. The tall blonde narrowed her eyes as she glared suspiciously at Anna. The woman looked to be a match for George, with her manicured nails and artfully drawn on makeup. "I think your date is waiting."

George looked over his shoulder. His smile was charming, and it was that impish look that got him both into and out of trouble. "Who? Carla, I mean *Darla*? Just say the word, and I'll leave her for you."

"We tried that, and it failed epically. So how long have you and Carla-Darla been dating?" Anna noticed the sharply jealous look on the woman's face. It wasn't unusual for George to stir up possessiveness in women. He had a natural charisma that assured he was never without company. Anna had briefly fallen for that charm. Never again. They were much better as friends.

"Um," George checked his phone clock. "Seven hours?"

Anna arched a brow and tried not to laugh. "What do you do? Pick them up as they pull into the hotel?"

"Hey, it's longer than Dr. Magnus knew his trophy wife before they married," George joked. "Besides, she's staying at a bed-and-breakfast."

Cassandra Magnus, or as some townsfolk jokingly called her, Candy Cane Magnum, was extremely beautiful, moderately nice, and not known for her intelligence and wit. But, Anna never felt the need to judge the woman or her marriage to the doctor. Happiness came in all forms.

As if summoned by their conversation Cassandra appeared in the doorway to the banquet room. Her platinum hair was sprayed higher than a

Texas pageant queen, and a pregnant belly had not dissuaded her from wearing a slinky, sequined gown.

"I love this time of year." George winked. "I see you brought the goods with you. Any chance I can score some of your special muffins?"

Anna sighed dramatically, pretending to be put out by his request. George laughed louder. She walked to the table holding the boxes of baked good she'd brought with her. They were marked with the Witch's Brew Coffee Shop and Bakery's logo. Everyone here probably knew who she was, but the constant advertising never hurt. It's how small businesses stayed in business. She reached into one of the boxes and took out two bite size cranberry-blueberry-nut muffins. Handing them to George, she said, "Stop calling them my special muffins. You make me sound like a drug dealer."

George popped them into his mouth and grinned as he backed away. "But they're so good, and I'm addicted."

"Anna Crawford?"

That voice again. The man had become more insistent. She turned her full attention once more to the stranger. "Yes. How can I help you?"

She didn't mean to sound exasperated, but it had been a long day, the first of a month full of unrelentingly long work days. If she left now, she could get four hours of sleep before getting up to make the banana nut bread, and should she do homemade yogurts with topping choices or cranberry cinnamon rolls or—

"My name is Jackson Argent." The words interrupted her train of thought.

Was she supposed to recognize him? A sudden worry entered her mind, and she didn't stop to think as she said, "Oh, no, did Polly send you to be my date tonight? She shouldn't have done that."

"I'm pretty sure there is an insult in that statement somewhere." This time he did smile, and the look was as attractive as she imagined it would be. "Why? Am I not your type?"

"I don't have any types," Anna said, a little flustered.

"Religiously inclined?"

"I'm busy," she corrected.

"I'm fascinated." His smile deepened.

Anna pressed her palm against her temple and shook her head. "I'm confused. How may I help you?"

"I'm a reporter. I wanted to introduce myself and ask you a couple of questions."

Now that explained the impression of restlessness she was sensing from him. Anna glanced around the empty front hall toward the voices coming from the banquet. "You're reporting on the old boys' club kick off to the Cranberry Festival? I'm not sure how hard-hitting the story of friends having an annual dinner will be, but knock yourself out. I'm sure they're full of tall tales and back-in-my-days." She gave a small laugh. "I'm the wrong person if you want a quote. I just deliver the baked goods."

"I have a feeling I'm talking to the right person." His eyes dipped over her.

Was he checking her out? Aside from a couple of the servers, the other women were in fancy gowns and heels. They were surely much more interesting to look at than Anna at work.

"You're the photographer who owns the coffee-slash-magic shop here in town," he stated as if she needed to be reminded.

"Just the coffee shop," she corrected. "Polly's Perfectly Magical Mystical Wondrous World of Wonders is all my Aunt Polly."

"Wondrous Wonders?"

"If you met Aunt Polly you'd understand," Anna answered. "And that's actually the shortened version of what she originally wanted to call it."

"What I was trying to say is I've seen your photography. You're—"

A loud feminine scream pierced the front hall, cutting him off. For a stunned moment, Anna stared at him and then glanced around. Chaos erupted in the banquet hall.

Jackson sprang into action and hurried toward the noise. Instinctively, she ran after him to see what had happened.

Darla shook violently. Her gown was disheveled as she stumbled out of the man's restroom. Pointing a shaky finger, the woman screamed intermittently, the sound stopping as she gasped between deafening cries to catch her breath. Darla's eyes stayed fixed on the restroom door as Talbot and Herbert tried to pull her away from what had frightened her.

A sick feeling unfurled in the pit of Anna's stomach, and she whispered, "no," as she continued forward. Sound seemed to fade. Time slowed, and she felt as if she walked through sludge. She leaned to look around the corner, first seeing the mask George had been carrying around that evening on the floor, and next to it a shoe.

Dr. Magnus pushed past her, jolting her to full awareness. Her hearing returned, bombarding her with the turmoil of the moment.

"Give them room. Back away," Herbert ordered as he herded the gathering crowd away from the restroom.

Anna knew who it was on the floor before she stepped fully into the scene.

George lay on the hard, cream-colored tile, his dress shirt had been ripped open and buttons lay scattered on the floor. She ignored the order to back away as she stood behind Dr. Magnus. George's body convulsed as Dr. Magnus tried to sweep green foamy liquid out of George's mouth to stop him from choking. A rash spread from George's lips down his neck and chest.

"George?" she whispered. Anna reached down to touch the doctor's shoulder, trying to energize his efforts with whatever natural magic she had in the hope of saving a friend. Since she'd spent so long suppressing her powers, it didn't appear to do much good.

For a second, she saw George's eyes twitch toward her and then he stopped moving.

"Ambulance is on its way," Herbert announced.

Anna pulled her hand off Dr. Magnus. She looked around in confusion, unable to believe what had happened. Blue lines ran across the walls, leading her gaze from the restroom stalls to where Jackson stood in the doorway watching her.

"Call the sheriff," Dr. Magnus said. "Have her send out one of the deputies to take a report." Then, as if out of habit, he glanced at his watch and said, "Time of death, 10:17 p.m."

"George?" Ginger screamed from somewhere within the banquet room as news of her son reached her. "No, George!"

Someone tugged on Anna's arm, pulling her back, away from the body.

"Come out of there," Judge Talbot told her. "This is no place for a lady."

Anna focused on the confusion around her. Ginger appeared, fighting to no avail to reach her boy. A red wine stain looked as if she'd spilled the drink down the side of her sleeveless light green dress in her panic. Darla cried and fanned herself in a corner as if she'd just lost the love of her life.

"What is happening?" someone asked. "Was an ambulance called?"

"He's so young," another added. "How could something like this happen?"

"Darling? What happened?" Cassandra asked her husband, her face pale with shock as she held her pregnant stomach.

"My baby," Ginger cried.

"We'll know more later, but it appears to be anaphylactic shock," Dr. Magnus said to his wife. He gently motioned that she should back away. "For now, it looks like an accident. He had a severe allergic reaction to something. Please, go sit. Stress is not good for the baby."

Ginger was incoherent as she tried to speak.

"Allergic reaction? I wonder if it was something he ate?" Jackson suddenly appeared next to her.

Anna glanced toward her boxes of food, not liking the implication of his words, whether he intended to accuse her or not. She didn't answer. Her mind fought between numbed shock and disbelief.

"I've never seen an allergic reaction show as green foam before," Jackson continued.

"There is no story here," Anna stated. "Please leave us in peace."

She moved toward Ginger who instantly grabbed hold of her and hugged her tight. Anna glanced over the shaking woman's shoulder. She tried to murmur soothing words but knew Ginger didn't hear them in her shocked state. Jackson still watched her, and she imagined his gaze was knowing and suspicious. There was nothing she could do about that now.

Chapter Four

"Yup, looks like an accident." Detective August, as he was called for his placement in the Everlasting sheriff department's yearly law enforcement calendar, spent all of four minutes on his investigation. That wasn't counting the forty-five minutes it took him to arrive. He was one of twelve men Sheriff Francine Bull had hired to round out the police department, not that Everlasting really needed that big of a force most of the year. The supernatural had a way of policing themselves. Although, the festival brought with it a surge of misdemeanors and speeding tickets. All of Bull's calendar boys were attractive, which, rumor had it, was the reason they'd made the final cut. August was no different with his green eyes, black hair, and a physique that took more hours in a gym than Anna spent working each week (which said a lot).

Detective August didn't have the best reputation as far as law enforcement was concerned. Anna had heard some of the other officers making jokes behind his back about his lack of experience and how it didn't stop the overly ambitious man from trying to get ahead in his career, in record time no less. They even speculated that he had blackmailed a public official.

It was almost insulting that he was the one who showed up for George.

"I see no reason to question your findings. Send me your official report, doc, and I'll write it up." August slapped his hand on Dr. Magnus' upper arm. "Case closed."

Anna gasped at the incompetence of the man, shocked at what she'd just witnessed. She wanted to protest, but found herself speechless.

"So, you don't think that green foam around his lips is suspicious and worth taking a deeper look?" Jackson asked.

August frowned in annoyance. "Are you a doctor?"

"Reporter," Jackson said.

At that admission, August squared his shoulders readying himself as if he was about to be inter-viewed on the nightly news. "Well, you see, what we have here is a clear tragedy. George Madison was a well-liked member of our community, and—"

"So, no thoughts of foul play? Poisoning?" Jackson interrupted.

"As much as I would like there to be a murd…" August began, before lowering his head and clearing his throat. "There is nothing suspicious. That's all for now." He pushed Jackson's shoulder to move past him as if the reporter was just one of a great mob trying to get him to talk. The detective strode from the lodge, motioning that the paramedics should get to work.

"How in the hell did that man make the rank of detective?" Jackson muttered. "I've seen better police work from a monkey in a costume."

"Ole August looked good in a thong is my guess," Mrs. London answered as she walked past.

Jackson automatically turned to watch the detective and gave a small shake of disgust as if he mentally pictured the woman's words.

"She's not wrong," Anna said, coming next to him.

"Did she say thong?" Jackson arched a brow.

"You heard right. It's all about the calendar. He's August. Thus we call him August," Anna said.

"Does August have a real name?" he asked.

"I'd assume so, but I never bothered to learn it." Anna couldn't believe this evening was happening. She wanted to rewind time and start over. "August is an idiot, but I trust Dr. Magnus. If there is something amiss with the death, he'll say so when he does his official examination. Please, drop it. There's no story to investigate here. Just sadness. Everyone liked George."

His eyes narrowed at the comment. He didn't believe her. She didn't care.

"Leave this alone." Anna watched the paramedics as they rolled their gurney out of the front door. Ginger walked behind them, held up by her arms as a couple of friends escorted her out.

Anna took her time gathering her belongings, not wanting to see the ambulance on the drive home. She felt tired as if the wind had been knocked out of her. One moment her biggest concern was baking banana nut bread, and the next...

Poor George. It's not fair.

"Do you need help carrying your bags to the car?" Jackson offered.

"No thank you," she dismissed, wanting to be alone. Her words were more of an autopilot answer, as she said, "Have a nice rest of your visit to our town, Mr. Argent."

As she finally drove back to her apartment above the coffee shop, a drizzle of light rain hit her windshield. She imagined them to be the tears she was unable to shed. Time seemed to skip as she made the drive home. Anna didn't own a car and preferred to ride her bike. The 1970 pink Cadillac belonged to Polly and ran like it was powered by magic and not actual mechanics. It clanged and vibrated and was twenty years overdue for a tune up at Jolene Bail's service station. Polly loved the car and kept it running with spells. She had customized the tan and black leather interior so that it sparkled.

At one point, she had a disco ball hanging in the back, but Anna made her remove it after she nearly blinded a passing driver. Glancing down at the keys, she shook her head. A tiny disco ball keychain hung from the ignition. There was no keeping Polly down.

The Cadillac sputtered as she pulled into town and began to lose power. It was all Anna could do to ease it into Jolene's service station parking lot. Putting the car in park, she leaned her head against the skinny steering wheel. This night needed to be over.

It was late, but on the off chance she'd catch Jolene working, she ran through the rain to the front door and pressed her face against the window to peek inside. Anna liked Jolene and always thought she'd make the perfect significant other for Wilber. There was just something incredibly sweet about the way the woman's face lit up when Wilber was around.

Since this wasn't the first time she'd had to coast Polly's car into the parking lot in the middle of the night, Anna knew where the hide-a-key was and let herself in. It took a couple of trips in the rain to bring all the boxes of goodies inside, but she was sure Jolene would appreciate the surprise on her front counter in the morning. The woman especially loved the cranberry scones' recipe when Anna used a little nutmeg.

Jolene's office had the faint smell of motor oil. A collection of antique oil cans was displayed on the shelf. Jolene had inherited the cans, and the business, from her father. The desk was piled with paperwork along one side. Anna found a piece of paper and jotted a quick note about Polly's car and the baked goods, thanking Jolene in advance for allowing her to leave the car parked at an angle in her lot. She placed the keys to the Cadillac on the note, took a garbage bag to cover her camera bag to protect it from the rain, and made sure to shut off all the lights and lock up before leaving the key where she'd found it.

Anna carried the camera bag and her purse inside the plastic bag as she made the trek home. The rain was light, but she had a feeling the storm would pick up soon. The moisture plus the breeze caused her to shiver. A few cars passed, but no one stopped. It was just as well, she wasn't in the mood for company.

One trudging step at a time, she made it to the coffee shop. Tourists still walked the street. The woman who worked for Anna, Marcy Lewis, had already closed up for the evening, so she used the alley door to the kitchen to go inside. If she opened the front, she was worried customers would flood in and try to make it an after hours party. Anna had considered opening 24-hours during the festival but knew she needed to sleep at some point.

Without turning on any of the downstairs lights, she went up the stairs to her small apartment. She sensed Polly was there before she even opened the door. White candles were lit all around the apartment, and the lights were off. She didn't bother to reach for the light switch.

Polly rushed in from the kitchen. She held a cup of steaming liquid. By the smell, Anna knew she didn't want to ask what it was.

"Hey, Polly." Anna set down the garbage bag and pulled out her camera to make sure it was still dry. "Your car died. I left it at Jolene's."

"I'll fix it first thing in the morning," Polly said.

"Or you can let Jolene do her job," Anna countered.

"My magic fingers have been keeping that beautiful beast running just fine," Polly dismissed. "She only acts up when you borrow it."

"Suit yourself." Anna yawned. She wanted to take a shower and fall into bed. "What are you doing here so late? Did the garden gnomes finally revolt and take over your house?"

Polly's expression turned grave. "At 10:17 I was giving Herman a bath when we felt a force leave

Everlasting. We were worried about you. We came right over."

Anna began to nod before furrowing her brow. Herman was Polly's enchanted pet lobster. "We?"

"You didn't want a bath, did you? I'm letting him spend the night in your tub," Polly said. "He was pretty upset. You know animals can sense things people can't."

Anna couldn't find the energy to have this conversation right now.

"Who was it?" Polly asked.

Anna didn't answer. Tears threatened and choked her voice.

"George." Polly shook her head sadly. "I was worried that was it. I didn't want it to be true. This makes no sense. I should have seen that in his cards. It was not his time. Something must have disrupted his natural flow. Would you like me to get out the tarot cards and do a reading? Or the spirit board so we can talk to him?"

"Not now, Polly." Anna couldn't deal with her aunt's special brand of crazy at the moment. She carried the camera bag into the bedroom she'd converted into a darkroom and shut the door. Polly knew not to come in while Anna was developing. Once alone in the dark, Anna slid onto the floor and rested her forehead on her knees. She wanted to erase this night from ever happening.

Chapter Five

George's funeral proved just how well liked he was. The town festival being in full swing didn't stop business owners from closing their stores to pay their last respects to their favorite delivery man. Arrangements of lilies, irises, daisies, and every other flower imaginable were snapped up by mourners and used to create wreaths, crosses, and standing sprays, which fragranced the thick air and added beauty to the tragic event.

Mrs. Mays sang an old hymn as the crowd departed. Her vibrato voice flowed over the cemetery like a magical mist. The Sunday school teacher wore the same collection of wide brim hats, white gloves, and Sunday dresses since Anna was a child. The woman looked genuinely upset by George's passing, as they all were.

A light breeze traversed the tombstones and

edifices of the dead. It cooled Anna as she began the long walk home. Usually, she would have ridden a bike, but that hardly seemed appropriate in her solemn black dress. Polly's Cadillac was still parked at Jolene's. The woman had finally offered to work on it for free if only to put the machine out of it's sputtering misery. Polly took that to mean the car had spoken to Jolene magically and had needs only a mechanic could attend to. She let Jolene work on the car, so long as she accepted multiple sage cleansings and blessings on her business in return.

Anna put distance between herself and the burial spot. Groups of people still hung near the graveside to pay respects. Others drove off in their cars, leaving the gloomy cemetery.

"How you doing, sweetheart? We all know how much you loved ole George." Judge Talbot tried to lay a hand on her shoulder, but Polly instantly appeared between the two of them. The judge had on a dark suit, which wasn't a huge change from his everyday attire. He liked to dress like he was still on his way to court, even though he hadn't sat on the bench for years.

"It was a lovely service, wasn't it, Anna?" Polly slipped her arm through Anna's and kept her close just as she had when Anna was a child. Funerals were the rare time Polly wore a somber color, out of respect of those mourning. "Don't you agree, Dougie?"

"You know that you are the only one that can get away with calling me Dougie," Judge Talbot said. Anna did not appreciate the flirtatious tone to his voice. This was hardly the time or place.

"It's nice that so many people came out to support George," Anna managed, more to Polly than to the judge.

"He was well liked," Polly agreed.

"A lot of women here," Talbot observed.

Anna couldn't help glancing around. There were a lot of women there, some she recognized from Everlasting and neighboring towns, most of them looked like tourists. Even George's seven-hour date, Carla-Darla, was there, dramatically fanning her cheeks and trying not to cry. No surprise, Darla was the kind of woman who dressed up for a funeral, with extra thick mascara and eyeliner so that she could dab delicately at her eyes and everyone could see how sad she was. Her black gown looked more suited for a cocktail party than a graveside service as did her high heels. She carried sunglasses but did not put them on, even when the sun shone in her eyes because that would have hidden the visible effect of her grief. The woman disgusted Anna with her attention seeking.

Anna caught a familiar face watching her from near the graveside. Jackson wore the same expression he'd had the night of the accident, watchful and curious. He looked handsome in his burgundy cashmere and black slacks, and for a moment, Anna couldn't look away. "What's he doing here?"

"Who?" Polly glanced around to see who Anna was talking about. "That handsome man who's been staring at you for the last hour?"

For some reason, the idea that Jackson had been watching her didn't cause the adverse reaction she would have expected. He was as ruggedly handsome as she remembered with his almost brooding expression. When she didn't pull her gaze away from him, he tilted his head in acknowledgment. She automatically returned the gesture. What did she care if this guy wanted to come to the funeral? There was no news story here, just a tragedy. Or was there? The events of the past forty-eight hours had taken their toll. A generally clear-headed person, Anna was finding it hard to think straight, let alone get her head around the death of her friend.

"I remember him," Talbot said. "He came to the banquet."

"He's a journalist," Anna answered. "He thinks there is a question about the way George died."

"I thought it was an allergic reaction," Talbot dismissed. "Must not be that good of a reporter. No mystery there."

"Did you hear about Ginger?" Hamilton joined them on the sidewalk, also wearing the ceremonial dark grays and blacks. "Poor thing had a breakdown. She was mumbling nearly incoherently about all the grandchildren she'll never have. Magnus gave her a sedative, and he and Cassandra are driving her home."

"That's right. George was the last of her family," Talbot said. "I noticed Captain Tom wasn't here today."

"I heard they broke up," Hamilton said. Anna usually liked the professor, but this conversation felt a little too much like gossiping.

"Not surprising, knowing Tom," Talbot said. "That man never was one to stick around through the hard times."

"Polly," Anna whispered. "Are you ready to go?"

"I'm very sorry, Anna. We all thought you and George…" Hamilton let his words trail off.

Anna shifted uncomfortably on her feet. "We were friends." She felt numb, still unable to believe George was gone.

"Anna, our ride is waiting, and you have a shipment expected at the store that you need to sign for." Polly tugged on her arm and nodded her head at the men in dismissal. "Gentlemen."

The men said their goodbyes as Polly led Anna to a nearby Nissan. The red car looked brand new and wasn't one she recognized. The sleek lines were a far cry from the metal tank of the classic Cadillac.

"Polly, did you buy a new car?" Anna asked.

"No." Polly opened the door to the back seat and motioned Anna to get in. The beige cloth seats still carried the new car smell. Anna leaned to look at the front seat for a clue as to who owned the car when she noticed there was a rental sticker on the front window. It wasn't like Polly to rent a car. If anything, Polly would have called her friend Captain Petey Winters to give her a ride on his motorcycle, well, more to the point in the sidecar attached to his motorcycle. Anna was pretty sure Petey had a crush on her aunt, but he never actually made his intentions fully known. Anna liked to tease her aunt about it, hoping she would pick up on the clues, but there was no way she was going beyond that to play matchmaker between the two.

"Polly, whose car is this?" Anna asked.

As if to answer the question, Jackson appeared. He gave them a quizzical look, glancing at Anna in the back seat and then at Polly starting to climb into his car. "Hello, ladies, can I help you?"

"Yes," Polly answered. "To the Witch's Brew Coffee Shop and Bakery, young man, straightaway and forthwith, and no talking. She doesn't need any more conversation."

"Yes, ma'am," Jackson answered. He took his place in the driver's seat and didn't speak as he drove them from the cemetery to the coffee shop.

The traffic was heavy from tourists and festival goers. Not to mention streets that were closed because of the event. Anna and Polly knew the shortcuts, but they passed up the chance to correct

Jackson's route to make the trip faster. Choosing instead to sit in silence.

Anna met his eyes through the rearview. He didn't know her history with George, and that gave her some sense of comfort. She liked that he wasn't currently looking at her with pity or questions.

Outside the window, the passing crowds moved in waves down Main Street's sidewalk. As they pulled in near the *Witch's Brew*, she saw Aaron Moore in front of the shop placing an assorted tray of muffins on a table next to a large bucket of bottled water. She studied the tray, noting that he had an abnormally high amount of the bran muffins in the selection. Not surprising, the young man had a stack of his band's CDs next to the shop's goods. Aside from his apron, he dressed as if he were about to go out on stage—skinny jeans, plaid shirt, and old cowboy hat. He liked to talk with a Texas accent though Anna knew from his employee interview and paperwork that he'd been born and raised in Pennsylvania.

Since Aaron was manning the street booth that meant Marcy would be inside running the counter. The place looked packed.

"Maybe we should go to my house," Polly offered. "You don't need this today."

"No, I need to keep busy." Anna leaned forward in her seat. "Thank you for the ride. You can let me out here. There will be nowhere for you to turn around with the roads blocked off ahead."

"You're welcome," Jackson said. "Anytime."

"Stop by the shop sometime. I owe you a coffee and croissant." Anna reached for the door handle.

"You don't owe me anything." Jackson gave her a small smile. "I'm happy to be of service."

Anna stepped into the sunlight and took a deep breath. The noise of passersby invaded her thoughts, and she ducked her head as she navigated her way inside the shop. Aaron waved as she passed by. He sang a few lyrics from one of his songs to a gathering crowd of college-age girls. They giggled and flirted at his attention.

"I'll help the children in the shop," Polly said. "You go on upstairs and have a cup of tea."

"I'm out of tea," Anna said. "I forgot to go to the grocery store."

"You live over a coffee shop. I'll bring you a cup."

"I can't," Anna protested. "Aaron has too many bran muffins on his tray. Those don't sell as well to this crowd. Which means we might be running low of the best sellers and I need to get on making more. Plus, Marcy probably needs an extra set of hands at the front counter. We need—"

A round of laughter cut off Anna's words. Marcy was waving her arms as she entertained the people waiting in line with her vivacious charm.

The woman was a walking vat of trivial knowledge and had a way with people.

"It looks like Marcy is doing just fine to me. She's got this. I'll make sure Aaron puts out a better variety. Now go." Polly gave her a gentle shove toward the door leading upstairs to her apartment.

"Fine, but let Marcy do the baking. You stay away from the food." Anna didn't protest again. The idea of talking to people and smiling held no appeal. All she wanted was to lay in bed and sleep.

Chapter Six

"How can I help you?" Anna didn't look up from the order she was working on as she detected another customer stepping up to the counter. Cosmically, it seemed right that Marcy had not shown up to work since Anna had pretty much abandoned the woman the day before.

"I need a photographer for the Cranberry Festival."

Anna's hands faltered, and she dropped a chocolate mint cookie on the floor. For some reason, the sound of the reporter's voice instantly drew her back two days to George's funeral when he'd given them a ride. A small wave of grief washed over her, and she took a deep breath. "We have coffee, a variety of scones, and if you're feeling adventurous Aunt Polly will read your tarot cards. I can personally recommend the first two, and the third you order at your own risk."

"But I need a photographer," he repeated. "And from what I can tell you're the best in the area."

At the compliment, she finally glanced up. "Turn around."

He obeyed. She couldn't help it as her eyes roamed down over him to check him out. The tight blue jeans did absolutely nothing to hide the attractive assets beneath. He wore a faded black 1980s band t-shirt that looked as if had seen several washings. Strangely, the relaxed look made him all that more appealing. Not to say he didn't look good in cashmere and business slacks, but there was something primal about a handsome man in jeans and a t-shirt.

"See all those millennials taking pictures of their chocolate chip fudge muffins and typing their hashtag Everlasting, hashtag Witch's Brew, hashtag yum? They're all photographers. I'm sure you can sweet talk them out of a dozen festival photographs." Anna picked the cookie off the floor and tossed it into the trash before washing her hands.

"I need a photographer, not a teenager with a camera phone." Jackson leaned against the counter. "I can pay."

"Even if I wanted to, I don't have time." She gestured toward the busy shop.

"You should hire help," he suggested. "I bet one of these millennials is looking for work."

"I have help. Or, I did. Aaron is out of town for a gig, and Marcy didn't show up for work today. It's not the first time. Her boyfriend probably did something either incredibly sweet or incredibly stupid." Anna dumped coffee grounds in the trash can and started another large pot.

"Why don't you fire her?" Jackson asked. "If someone consistently misses a shift, it would make sense that they didn't keep their job."

That's not how Anna did business. She trusted her instincts. Plus, Marcy was a great worker and could be trusted completely. "The bonus about Marcy is that when she does come back, she'll feel so guilty she'll work extra hard. Regardless, none of that helps me today since I don't think she's coming in." Anna leaned to the side to look at the young redheaded woman standing behind Jackson. "Can I help you?"

"Skinny mocha soy latte with extra cream and chocolate sprinkles," the woman said. Her pixie cut emulated her energy. She bounced lightly on her feet and she waited as if her legs might suddenly burst into movement. She wore a baseball t-shirt from Warrick's Surf & Turf near the shore. The restaurant was very high end, not the kind of place that one would expect to find t-shirts, but she also knew he supported a local baseball team so it wasn't unheard of that the shirts would be for sale somewhere in town. Anna wondered if maybe she could make a profit from selling t-shirts for Witch's Brew. Curt Warrick was nothing if not a savvy businessman, proven by all the real estate he owned around Everlasting.

"One skinny mocha soy latte with extra cream and chocolate sprinkles coming up," Anna said.

"And are your cookies gluten-free?" the pixie asked.

"Gluten-free selections are on the right under the sign," Anna answered, as she worked on the latte order.

"I want your eye for detail," Jackson insisted, trying to pick up their conversation where it left off.

Anna paused long enough to pour him a cup of coffee and set it on the counter. "The coffee I owe you for the ride. Cream, sugar, and artificial sweeteners are to your right on the creamer bar."

"Thanks." He picked up the coffee cup and sipped it. "I like it black."

"You're welcome. If you give me just a second, I'll get a warm cinnamon raisin croissant for you. They are about to come out of the oven." She went back to work on the latte.

"I'm not giving up until you say yes. I need a photographer with your skill level." He took another sip and looked as if he had all the time in the world. "Is this a French Roast?"

"And I want to grow three more pairs of hands," she quipped, ignoring his coffee question.

"That one," the redhead said, pointing into the case.

"Why don't you like me?" Jackson inquired, his tone playful.

"Which one?" Anna placed the latte on the counter and leaned over to look where the redheaded pixie pointed.

"Is this going to be long? I'm in a hurry," a man insisted. He stood a few places back in the line. He had been glaring in annoyance since he'd walked in the door. His business suit seemed out of place amongst the other tourists, and apparently he was convinced that his self-importance should be intimidating in and of itself.

"The snickerdoodle," the redhead said.

"We don't have snickerdoodle," Anna answered. How hard was it to read labels? Nowhere in her case was there a snickerdoodle.

"I meant peanut butter," the redhead corrected.

"Excellent choice," Jackson praised.

The woman gave him a flirty smile. "Thank you."

"I don't have time to take on a photo assignment. I'm sorry," Anna dismissed Jackson.

"I just need a coffee," the impatient businessman persisted. "How hard is it to grab a cookie? This isn't rocket science."

"Oh, for pity's sake." Without being invited, Jackson moved around the counter. He poured a large, plain coffee, and placed it on top of the display case. He pointed at the rude man and said, "You. That will be twenty-five dollars."

"But—?" the man began to protest the price.

"Jerk tax," Jackson said. "You want it or not? It's about to go up to thirty. As you said, people are waiting, and coffee is in high demand."

Several people in line chuckled. A few took pictures of what was happening and began typing furiously on their phones.

"Forget it." The man left without purchasing anything. He stormed out of the coffee shop.

Anna took the redhead's payment. "Excuse me. I need to grab more coffee beans." She pushed Jackson through the kitchen door into the back. When they were out of sight of her customers, she said, "What do you think you're doing? This is my livelihood."

"That guy was a jerk," Jackson dismissed. "I didn't like the way he was talking to you."

"And who are you to decide how people can talk to me?" Anna demanded.

"Maybe I'm your knight in shining armor." He grinned. Was he flirting with her? Now? Here?

"Do I look like a damsel in distress?" She placed her hands on her hips. "Jerks are a part of running a business. There will be twelve more of him this morning alone."

Jackson lost his smile. "You're really mad, aren't you?"

She rubbed the bridge of her nose. "You think I don't want to tell the jerks off? If I treated them all like that, I'd stop making money. Piss enough of them off, and I cease to be the must-go-to place for coffee during the festival, to a place that people avoid because some idiot I offended decides to lie and say I gave him food poisoning. They'll all end up at Chickadee's Diner or the local gas station."

"I only wanted to lend a hand. You looked like you need it, and I thought if I helped you catch up on your work you'd assist me with mine," he said.

Anna sighed. Polly was supposed to be helping out this month, but she'd disappeared upstairs into Anna's apartment with a handful of sage to cleanse the home of negative energy. Yesterday, Polly had insisted she had to find Hugh Lupine, owner of the Full Moon Fishing Charter, to aid him in ending a curse to win a bet—whatever that meant. The day before that was the funeral, and Anna had caught Polly trying to séance George…again. Before that, she simply forgot to show up because Herman the lobster needed to talk. Anna knew Polly took her witchcraft very seriously, and couldn't be mad at her when she disappeared like she did. For all her eccentricities, Polly truly believed she kept balance in the world.

"Behave. No jerk taxes. Be nice to my customers. And you better know what you're doing because I won't hesitate to fire you." Anna pointed to the counter. "Now restock the cookie case and put more of the banana nut muffins on the display stand. Then, make sure the coffee condiment bar has enough of those individual creamers and butters. We're usually starting to run low this time of the morning."

"Yes, boss," Jackson answered as if this kind of thing happened to him every day. She supposed as a reporter he was used to handling new situations.

The oven timer began to beep. "Croissants are done. Pull them out for me, please, so they can cool a little."

"As you wish." Jackson bowed and winked at her. He went toward the oven and stared at it for a second before turning off the timer.

Anna tried her best not to give in to his flirtation and held back her smile. "Don't make me regret this."

Chapter Seven

"Argent, you say? I knew a Billy Argent. Went by the name Bad Billy." Anna's Aunt Polly had clearly outdone herself in a yellow polyester dress and bright red shoes. Though her style would have looked almost clownish on anyone else, the little spitfire somehow carried it off. It was an amplification of who she was.

Jackson found he liked Polly. She had an infectious personality, both flighty and caring, that seeped from every word and gesture. Her thoughts moved like water, changing subjects like the ebb and flow of the tides.

"My father was William Argent," Jackson admitted. It was hard for him to acknowledge the man here, in this town. His family history wasn't exactly brag-worthy.

"That explains your little trick," Polly said

knowingly, giving him a wink. "You're not planning on robbing the place, are you?"

Jackson tried to be offended, but couldn't. There was something to Polly's expression that said she didn't judge him. "I wouldn't dream of it."

"Too bad," Polly laughed. "There is one thing I'd like to see you steal." She gave a meaningful glance at her niece as Anna joined them from the kitchen.

"You mean those chocolate caramel scones?" he teased.

Polly arched a brow. "You don't do subtle, do you? I'm talking about my niece. I'd like you to steal my niece's attention. She needs a date, and I think you two are cute together."

Jackson suppressed his laugh.

"That was some day." Anna went to lock the front door. Though he'd seen firsthand how hard she worked, she didn't show her exhaustion. She'd taken off her work apron. She wore a peach-colored tunic top with long sleeves and cross laces over the chest. When she lifted her hand to flip the sign in her window to indicate they were now closed, he received an enjoyable view of just how tightly her black leggings hugged her hips.

Before Jackson had arrived that morning to hire her, he'd almost convinced himself that she could have been George's murderer. He'd spent almost the entire day after the funeral in his hotel room pouring over the facts and building a case to support his urge to investigate.

His journalistic instincts were tingling on this one. Dr. Magnus wrote George's death off as an accident, but Jackson wasn't buying it. He'd seen anaphylactic shock before. The symptoms didn't fit what he was finding online. What it did resemble, however, was a poisoning. That indicated murder.

Anna as a suspect made logical sense. He'd seen Anna give George something to eat moments before his death. Normally, he'd project his consciousness to follow her around without her knowing. But, with Polly's ability to see his supernatural skill, he couldn't depend on it to find his answers. He came to her planning to investigate Anna the hard way.

Then he spent the day with her. Logic didn't fit the way he felt when he was by her. Nothing about her said she would hurt another person. He'd seen her catch and release a spider that afternoon.

Anna dumped over the tip jar and began counting out its contents onto the counter. "What are you two in here talking about?"

"I was telling your Aunt that I enjoyed myself today," he said. "It's been a long time since I worked a regular job."

"Reporting's not normal?" Anna sounded distracted. Her mouth moved as she silently counted.

"Not if you do it right." Jackson chuckled.

"That's not what I was saying," Polly interrupted. "I was telling him that I wanted him to ask you out on a date. I have a good sense of this one, Anna. You should say yes when he does. If you're not sure what to do, I can ask Petey if you can use one of Hugh's fishing boats. Nothing more romantic than being out on the water."

"Oh, OK, Aunt Polly." Anna rolled her eyes as if that wasn't the first time her aunt had been so bold. She picked up the stack of tips and began recounting it into a pile.

"Then we can double date," Polly added.

"OK, Pol—what, wait, who are you dating?" Anna stopped counting and eyed her aunt. "Why are you all dressed up tonight? Where are you going? Did you finally say yes to Captain Petey?"

"Who's this Captain Petey?" Jackson asked, curious as he enjoyed the interplay between the women.

"A very prominent businessman," Polly said. "We've been friends since the dinosaurs ate the cavemen."

"He owns Worm and Wonder, a bait and tackle store on the waterfront," Anna explained. "I'm pretty sure his idea of a romantic date is to bring a woman a corsage made out of fishing lures, before taking her on a tour of a worm farm."

"He is romantic at heart," Polly agreed. "Such a sweetie."

"Yes," Anna nodded. "He's been wooing Polly by bringing her his catch of the day—"

"That sounds nice," Jackson inserted diplomatically.

"—and slapping newspaper wrapped fish on my coffee counter during business hours. I know we're trying to promote the image of a quaint fishing village, but I don't exactly want the smell of a cannery in here when I'm trying to sell chocolate croissants to tourists."

"Petey has not once asked me out. We're just friends. It is very sweet," Polly told Jackson. "He gave me Herman."

"Herman?" Jackson prompted.

"My pet lobster," Polly explained.

"A pet lobster, of course," Jackson said. Somehow that didn't surprise him.

"Unfortunately, Petey did not have that one wrapped up in a newspaper," Anna told Jackson. "Herman didn't have his pinchers restrained. He tried to clip the fingers off of one of my customers."

"Of course, Petey didn't put him in a newspaper," Polly said. "Lobsters have their gills on their underbellies, and they need water to breathe. Petey had him in a mini swimming pool."

"What happened to the customer?" Jackson looked from aunt to niece and then back again.

"She screamed like aliens were attacking. A little dramatic if you ask me. Everyone knows aliens are green," Polly dismissed any concern. "Herman couldn't help it. He was scared. I for one am glad his pinchers weren't tied. How would you like it if someone dropped you into the ocean with your fingers bound together?"

"Your aunt has a point," Jackson said with a smirk as he tried not to laugh.

"I think Petey expected you to eat Herman," Anna said, "not make him little shirts and push him around in a wagon full of water."

"Nonsense," Polly dismissed. "He was in a mini swimming pool. He is a pet."

"That wasn't a pool. It was a casserole dish," Anna clarified.

"I have to meet this lobster." Jackson was utterly fascinated.

"You will. I tried to release him back into the wild, but he followed me along the beach. Herman wanted to be with me, so I took him home. I have a tank, so he doesn't get too hot or cold, but on nice days I let him play outside in the pond. He even comes here to work with me. I'm teaching him how to bake."

Jackson looked at Anna for verification.

"No, you don't bring a lobster into my sterile kitchen where I bake for customers," Anna said, her tone dropping with worry.

"Oh, ah, yeah, no," Polly said unconvincingly. "I mean, *noooo* I wouldn't do that."

Anna arched a brow. "Herman can't work here."

"Of course not," Polly giggled. "Lobsters don't get paychecks."

Anna counted a few more bills and then took what was left in her hand to Jackson.

"What's this for?" He hesitated as he took the money. He hadn't expected to be paid.

"Your half of the tips," she said. "You earned it."

"I don't—" Something about her direct look cut off his words of protest, and he slipped the bills into his pocket. "Thank you."

"You'll never find a man being so picky," Polly resumed the conversation about dating as if they had never digressed. "But, for your information, no Captain Petey did not ask me out on a date. As I've told you a thousand times, we're just friends. He is partaking of his nightly whiskey at the Magic Eight Ball, and you know I don't like to interrupt a good ritual. I'm going to see Cornelius. Tonight, is the night he's finally going to reveal himself to me. I can feel it."

"Who's Cornelius?" Jackson asked, riveted by his peek into the life of these two women. They completely captivated him with their fluid banter.

"Don't ask," said Anna.

"A very interesting man," Polly answered.

"Isn't he married?" Anna teased.

"Not anymore. 'Til death he did part. He haunts the lighthouse." Polly gave her niece a playful wink before continuing, "and tonight is the night he's going to manifest for me."

Anna began lifting chairs upside down and placed them so that the backs hung over the edge of the tables in preparation of cleaning the floors. Jackson helped her, following her lead.

"Polly, I love you," Anna went into the kitchen and returned with a vacuum, "but sometimes I think you're one Hanged Man short of a tarot deck."

"Cornelius is dead?" Jackson clarified. "You're going on a ghost hunt?"

"It's tragic, really, sweet Cornelius was betrayed by his wife and cousin," Polly explained, dramatically using her hands to narrate the story. "Now he's doomed to roam the lighthouse forever. He can't ever leave it."

"All this without pants, apparently," Anna added wryly.

"I'd like to see this ghost," Jackson said.

"Nope, sorry, he only shows himself to women." Polly went to the bakery case and began pulling out cookies.

"Not all women," Anna goaded her aunt. "He won't show himself to Polly."

"He's shy," Polly explained. "It's an admirable quality in a man."

"You're bringing cookies to the ghost? I mean, they're delicious, and I like chocolate chip double fudge mint as much as the next guy, but do you think it will tempt a ghost to manifest?" Jackson took the cord from the vacuum and plugged it in.

"No, these are for Sapphire, the lady who lives in the lighthouse." Polly reached into a jar labeled organic cat treats and began scooping them into a small bag.

"And the cat food?" he inquired.

"Sapphire has cats," Polly answered as if it should have been obvious. "Oh, and before I forget, careful with your new camera, Anna. I hear the FOL are in town, and if they learn you have something from Wil's place they'll want to take a look at it."

"Who?" Anna frowned. She gave Jackson a sidelong glance as if trying to communicate silently to Polly that she needed to be quiet.

"I told you about them. The Fraternal Order of Light is always trying to get into Wil's place to confiscate his collection of unique items." Polly gave a small laugh. "I helped him strengthen his warding against the Collective last week. Wil's family has been looking after those things for centuries. No safer place."

Jackson had no idea what they were talking about.

"Polly," Anna warned in a low tone.

"Oh, fiddle-faddle with your worrying. Jackson's cool. We can talk in front of him. He knows all about the supernatural. His family is from Everlasting," Polly said.

Anna glanced at Jackson. He nodded, confirming it.

Polly grinned as she moved toward the shop door. "Don't wait up."

"I never do," Anna answered. When they were alone, her eyes didn't readily meet his. "You'll have to excuse Polly. She's a—"

"Hopeless romantic?" Jackson supplied.

"A nut," Anna corrected. "But I love her. She's my nut. I also think Petey has a crush on her he's never told her about, but Polly is oblivious to his true feelings. However, unlike my aunt, I don't meddle in the love lives of others."

"I think she's one of the most interesting people I've ever met," Jackson defended the eccentric lady. "Besides, I thought all good witches were supposed to march to their own drum."

"Did Polly tell you she was a witch?" Anna relocked the front door after her aunt.

"She didn't have to. Her little store back there makes it fairly obvious she's a witch." Jackson leaned against a table top and crossed his arms. "And you? Are you a witch, too?"

"That's a complicated question." Anna busied

herself cleaning and straightening sale items on the shelf near the register.

"How so? Will your coven get angry if you talk to me about it?" Jackson pushed up from the table and joined her by the display. Someone had browsed through the tea tins, and he started re-stacking them neatly for her.

"Polly and I don't belong to any of the local covens." She moved to fuss with the pottery display near the creamer bar.

"Sounds like there's a story in that statement." He followed her. "Does Polly not get along with the local covens?"

"They have different ideas on what magic is, but there has never been any trouble between them. A few of the other local witches were just in here asking Polly about some book they're trying to find, and I know Polly has helped them with potions in the past." She tapped her finger near the pottery as if silently counting it.

"I find Polly fascinating." Jackson smiled. Polly wasn't the only Crawford woman who fascinated him. "And you?"

"I try to stay out of the local covens' business. I know what I know, and I am who I am."

That's exactly what he wanted to figure out. Who was Anna Crawford, really? If Jackson paid attention to the facts, Anna could very well have poisoned her ex-boyfriend. He'd done some digging. Apparently, Anna and George had dated at one point. A few people even said George and Anna been engaged, but it had ended suddenly. Since George had been dating, they all assumed he was over it. As far as anyone knew, Anna was well on her way to becoming a lonely spinster and didn't date.

As Jackson now stood with her, alone in her coffee shop, watching her go through the motions of closing for the night, he couldn't see her as a murderer. In fact, all logic seemed to be flowing right out of his head, as if she cast as spell over him. It wouldn't be unheard of. They were in Everlasting, a mystical if not mysterious place.

Anna pointed toward the register. "Would you mind jotting down two creamers, six coffee cups, and a dozen tea cups on that notebook over there? I need to remember to ask Beatrice Park to make more. She's a local potter who supplies all my ceramics."

"Done." Jackson did as she asked. "So, is this Herman Polly's familiar or something?"

"Who knows? Polly said once that her familiar was a garden gnome living in her garden, but those are either made of concrete or plastic." Anna finished with the pottery shelf and moved to arrange the bottles of coffee flavoring.

"And you? Do you have a familiar?"

"What do you know about familiars?" She gave

him a pointed look as if he was asking about trade secrets.

"Only that they're a spirit animal connected to witches, and that every witch has one," he said. "Something like that?"

"Yeah, something like that," she chuckled softly.

"Well? Do you?" Jackson wanted to unravel the mystery she presented. He doubted she was playing coy on purpose.

"Like I said, it's complicated." She frowned thoughtfully at the shelf. "Do you think if I had t-shirts printed with my shop logo that people would buy them?"

"I would think so," Jackson said. "People seem to like vacation t-shirts, and a magical coffee bean would have broad appeal."

She looked around her shop, and he imagined she was contemplating other possible expansions.

"Polly seems to think we're cute together." He couldn't resist pointing it out and watched closely for her reaction.

"Polly likes to meddle."

"So, does that mean you don't want me to ask you out?" He tried to keep the seductive nature from being too obvious in his tone.

"Ignore Polly." Anna grabbed hold of the vacuum cleaner handle. "She believes a woman should always be in love. She says that a woman without love is like a jar of beetles without a queen."

Jackson frowned. "I don't think that makes sense. Ants in an ant farm, maybe."

"Things Polly says rarely make sense." Anna turned on the vacuum, ending the conversation.

Jackson watched her for a moment before wandering to look at her photographs, moving along the wall as if he were at a gallery. He found a picture of Polly holding a broom while wearing a conical hat. Carved pumpkin faces glowed behind her.

The vacuum stopped.

"Halloween?" he asked, not taking his eyes from the picture.

"My themed sixteenth birthday party," Anna said.

"Looks like fun." Jackson leaned closer, trying to make out a corner of the photo. The image was unclear, but it could have been a cat.

"Not pictured is Polly later streaking under the full moon, almost getting arrested, and me having to pick her up from the docks where she met a lovely bunch of Norwegian sailors."

"You pick up after her quite a bit, don't you?"

At that Anna paused, dropping the vacuum cord. "I wouldn't say that. When my parents died, she took care of me. There was no one else. If not for her, I'd have been shipped off to foster care to live with strangers. I'd say we take care of each other. What about you? What did Polly mean by her knowing your father?"

She had heard them talking about that?

"Do you want help with the vacuum?" he asked, diverting the subject of Bad Billy Argent. He quickly pulled the cord, looping it around his hand and elbow instead of using the built-in cord holder. He draped it on the handle and carried the vacuum cleaner toward the kitchen.

"You already said you're from here." She called behind him, not letting the subject drop. "Or at least your family is. What's the story there?"

Jackson looked around the clean kitchen and didn't move. There was a back door. He could escape. Closing his eyes, he projected himself back into the front of the coffee shop to watch Anna's face. She stared at the kitchen door as if waiting for him to return. He couldn't name the sentiment in her expression. It was almost sad, lonely. He crossed his consciousness over to her and lifted a ghostly hand to sweep past her cheek. Her eyes closed as if she felt him, but she gave no other indication that she knew what he was doing.

"Jackson?" she called. "Where did you go?"

He snapped his consciousness away from her and regained complete control of his body. "Coming." He set the vacuum against the corner away from the kitchen appliances and joined her once more in the front of the shop. "Is that everything?"

"Your family is from here?" she insisted. "And that is why you know things about…?"

"Supernaturals," he offered. "Yes, I know about supernaturals. That's why I wasn't worried when I found out your aunt is a natural witch, and that you most likely inherited the gene too—even though you say it's complicated. I also know that outsiders don't know what happens in this town. I'm not going to be the one to tell them if that's why you're asking. Even if I wanted to, no one but a few crazies would believe me, and I'd lose any journalistic credibility I have."

"I looked you up," Anna admitted. "It now makes sense why you're here. You must be visiting. I couldn't figure out why someone who spent so much time in Washington D.C. covering politics, in Oregon on environmental impact issues, and investigating oil spills and corporate corruption, would suddenly be interested in a cranberry festival. It's not like there is some scandal."

He thought of George. "My editor seems to believe there are mysteries here."

"I think we both know the types of rumors he's referring too," Anna said. "Like you said, you can't write about those. No one would believe you. As far as the rest of the world is concerned, we're nothing but fiction."

"What about murder?" he persisted. "Is that worth looking into?"

"If you know about this town, then you know that George's allergic reaction wasn't like most people's."

"That doesn't make it an accident," Jackson insisted. "People use allergies as a method to kill all the time."

"This isn't some crime drama episode," Anna scolded. "George was…*George*. He was well liked. No one ever had an ill word to say about him. Sure, he liked to joke around and pull pranks, but nothing that would warrant anyone wanting him dead. He's not rich, so it's not money. He doesn't own his own business, so there's no seedy business partner to want his cut of anything. He's not married and doesn't have a girlfriend, so no one to be jealous. No family besides his mother and I doubt she would want to cut him out of his inheritance. Why would anyone want to murder George? And then, to do that, they'd have to research him and figure out what he was allergic to."

"Or what his supernatural kind was allergic to," Jackson put forth. "What was he? Maybe someone had an issue with what he was, not who."

Anna's lips tightened as if her natural instinct was to hide the truth. He wasn't surprised. This was not a subject most residents would talk about openly. They were used to hiding their true selves, just like he was. Finally, she said, "His people are from a Nordic tribe of forest elves, known to be genetically blessed with good looks, charm, and being fertile. He is most literally a lover, not a fighter. Men, women, animals, they all like him. I have to believe this is a freak accident."

"What if it's not?" he insisted. "Don't you want to know for sure?"

"What makes you so sure it's not?" she countered. "Why don't you investigate the dead bodies washing up on shore? I hear the police are looking into that crime."

"Because, like you said, that's already being investigated by the police. George isn't. I tried talking to that Detective August, and he blew me off. He called me Fred and told me to crawl back into my Mystery Machine. The man actually said there were more important cases in town. As you deduced, George wasn't rich, wasn't a prominent businessman, and had no enemies. No person is that perfect, Nordic elf blood or not. I'm interested in what's not being investigated, or what's being covered up."

"If Dr. Magnus ruled George's death an accident, then Detective August has no reason to investigate." Anna gave him a pained look. "It's tragic, but—"

Jackson reached into his back pocket and pulled out his phone. "I read the autopsy report. Dr. Magnus ruled it accidental, but could not determine the cause of the anaphylactic shock." He scrolled through his photos before holding up a copy of the report. "Read it for yourself."

Anna frowned, even as she reached to look at the document. "How did you get this?"

"I'm good at my job," he answered. "Read it. Look at the notations. Green substance, unknown. Lab work, inconclusive evidence. Allergen, unknown. There are no signs of a struggle. Insufficient evidence to rule this as a homicide."

Anna slowly looked up as she returned his phone, "Stomach contents, cranberry baked goods and champagne. You think I did it because I gave him muffins, don't you? That's really why you're here. You don't need a photographer."

"Logically, you'd be a suspect, but my instincts tell me it wasn't you. I've learned to trust my intuition."

"Well, gee, thanks," she drawled sarcastically. "It's always nice to hear I don't come off as a murderer."

"And, for the record, just so we're clear. I do need a photographer. I really am assigned to cover the festival. Words are not compelling enough on their own to make people click for more, so I need unique images to keep my rankings up on the news sites. High clicks mean more by line exposure and more jobs. I'll give you credit of course, and I'll pay you."

"Fine. I'll do it," she said. "But the deal was you help me out here, and I'd help you out with photos."

Jackson smiled. "If you wish, but I wish you'd reconsider. It's not like the pay comes out of my pocket. It's on the company dime. Maybe you can use it for your first print run of Witch's Brew t-shirts."

"All right, maybe I'll take you up on that. I have plenty of unpublished photos you can choose from upstairs in my apartment." She motioned that he should follow her. "You can look while I make something to eat. I don't know about you, but I'm starving."

Chapter Eight

Anna hoped Jackson wasn't looking forward to a home-cooked meal as she took the prepackaged pizza out of the oven and began slicing it. Out of habit, she took a deep breath and said quietly to herself, "May whosoever partake of this meal be blessed with health, happiness, and good fortune." Frozen pizza and a bottle of zinfandel was the best she could do on short notice. It was either that or a stack of cookies from downstairs. She paused on her way out the door and turned back around to open her "special" seasoning cabinet. Anna didn't typically use it, but her aunt insisted she kept one in her apartment in case of magical emergencies.

A few drops of this, a couple sprinkles of that, and he'd be compelled to talk without a filter between his thoughts and his mouth. People always had secrets. Usually, Anna believed people should be allowed to keep them. She fingered a small jar, untwisting the cap on the red-tinted liquid.

"No," she whispered. Anna lived her life not depending on her natural magic. She wasn't about to start cutting corners with witchcraft now. She recapped the jar and put it back.

Anna was grateful her large two-bedroom apartment was at least picked up before she invited Jackson up. Well, not counting her messy desktop. Bookkeeping always seemed to be a distant afterthought during the busy season. Considering she lived alone, the size of the space was definitely a bonus as it ran the entire length of the second story. Painted gray brick made up the exterior walls while sheetrock rooms had been built into the long rectangular area. There wasn't much by way of soundproofing between rooms, but at least the noise from below was muffled by the wood floors, which were covered intermittently with brown and taupe shag rugs.

The décor was a mix of gifts and her simple, minimalist, shabby-chic tastes. The cat figurines and snow globes were all Polly. They seemed a kooky pairing with the black-and-white photos Anna had taken of the locals, but she wouldn't hurt her aunt's feelings by not displaying them. A low bookshelf filled with old paperbacks lined the length of the living room under the windows showing Main Street. It had been a long time since she'd stopped to read a book, but that didn't mean that someday she wouldn't be able to pick up the beloved hobby again.

In truth, she didn't spend much on her home. Every extra penny she had, she either saved or invested into expanding the coffee shop. Her two splurges had been her queen size bed and her living room couch. The memory foam mattress was a blessing after a very long, hard day at work. The beige couch she had purchased solely for the marshmallowy comfort. It was so big the delivery men had a heck of a time forcing it up the stairs. Deep red pillows were piled to one side from where she'd lain to watch movies on her laptop.

The living room and dining room had an open floor plan. Anna found Jackson at her small dining table, sorting through the photo proofs she'd laid out for him. He'd set several of them aside. Anna slid the pizza onto the table and pulled the wine bottle from under her arm. "Glasses are in the cabinet behind you."

Jackson turned and pulled out two stemless wine glasses at her suggestion.

"Any of these going to work for what you need? I like prints, but I have digital backups of everything." She sat and picked up a slice of pizza while he uncorked the wine. A loud shout sounded outside, reminding her they weren't alone in the world. The tourists were still out roaming the streets.

"I am so hungry. I forget to eat on busy days like this."

Jackson poured the wine and set a glass in front of her. He gestured at the pizza. "Are you sure this counts as food?"

"What?" She laughed. "Not gourmet enough for you?"

"I was teasing." Jackson gave her a playful grin. "I seriously can't judge. Most of my food comes from takeout boxes."

"Most of mine comes from the frozen food section of the grocery store." Anna took another bite. "Mmm, just like Aunt Polly used to make."

"I was right. You have an eye for detail." Jackson lifted a picture of hands destroying a row of cran- berry pies at the pie eating contest. "These should be in a fancy art museum, not on a news stream."

"I do a few odd jobs, weddings, and special events. It's hard to make money in photography these days. When I first started, it was darkrooms and film rolls. We had to know chemical baths, ventilation, and… Well, anyway, now everyone has a digital camera and beauty filters and fancies them- selves a photographer. It's never been an easy way to make a living, now it's become harder." Anna picked up a photo she'd taken of a couple of deputies patrolling the crowd. "This is a good one. The police around here like their picture taken."

"Is that the camera you were using the other

night?" Jackson inquired, gesturing to where she'd stored the antique camera on top of a bookshelf.

"Do you want to see the print? It's not perfect, but it turned out better than I expected considering I haven't played with the calotype process for years." She set down a slice of half-eaten pizza. After developing the photograph, she'd set it aside, unable to think of that night and her lost friend. She retrieved it from her darkroom and brought it to the table. She noticed he hadn't touched the pizza. "You don't like pepperoni?"

"Yeah, about that." Jackson stood and pulled the tip money out of his pocket. He placed it on the table. "I kind of ate a little of the inventory."

Anna arched a brow at his admission.

"Couple dozen cookies," he confessed. "One of those scones, a croissant, two Danishes, and a tart."

"OK, that's fine—"

"Three muffins," he continued, "and a mini cookie bag, a granola bar, and a slice of that banana nut bread, the pink yogurt…"

"You ate all that when I wasn't looking?" Anna couldn't help but laugh. "I guess I need to beef up security." Then, thinking of what he'd said, she laughed harder.

"It's not that funny, is it? I couldn't help it. They're delicious."

"I'm laughing because we don't have bags of mini cookies."

"Yes, you do. They're in the box on the kitchen counter."

Anna shook her head. "The green bags? Those are organic dog treats I made to donate to the animal shelter." His body stiffened as if he was trying to decide how to react. "But if it makes you feel better, they are completely people safe. Mostly peanut butter and yogurt."

"No, these bags were clear with pink ribbons," he answered, "and they tasted like chocolate."

"It was probably something of Polly's." Anna grimaced. "You're not feeling funny, are you? Little star bursts in your vision? A sudden need to be married? Craving marshmallows? Fear of silverware? An itch to gamble or raise chickens?"

"No. Not feeling the urge to get into the poultry trade." Jackson tilted his head in thought. "Though I did notice a strange patch of fur growing on my back and I can't quit thinking about the full moon."

Anna stiffened. "Dammit, Polly. How did you figure out how to make a werewolf?" She hurried toward the kitchen to look into the special cabinet. "Don't worry. I'm sure there is something here that will…"

"Anna, I'm teasing, there's nothing wrong with me." The sound of the wine bottle being poured drowned out some of his words. "I'm all right."

She leaned around the doorway to study him.

He was smiling at her as he raised the wine glass in a silent toast.

"That is more than the cost of baked goods," Anna said as she motioned toward the tip money scattered on the table.

"Donate it to the animal shelter," he suggested. "When you drop off the green bags."

"So, what do you think of the new camera?" Anna stood beside the table. The monochrome photograph's sepia tones were in shades of brown, rather than a more modern black-and-white grayscale. The edges were washed out, framing the image. The Sacred Order of Hairy Old Men looked like a scene from the distant past. Their masked faces and business suits emulated some ole boys' club from the turn of the century. All of the faces were in decent focus except for one. "I didn't notice that before. George must have moved during the exposure time. He turned out blurry."

"What's that behind him?" Jackson leaned closer to the print.

Anna picked up the photo and set it beneath a lamp. "It looks like some kind of face. Maybe a water spot or part of the chemical reaction process from the darkroom?"

"No, it's a person, look closer." He traced his finger over a shape. "There, it's the curve of a hip."

"Maybe I messed up the development process,"

she said. "There were no women in the frame, and I treated the paper myself."

"A ghost image?" Jackson wondered aloud. "I've heard stories of cameras that can capture images of the dead. Where did you get that camera?"

"From Wil at the antique shop. He's had it since I can remember. He gave it to me as a gift." Anna thought about the card that had come with it.

I haven't been able to sell it to you, for things like this should never be sold, but I must find it a new caretaker as it grows restless to be used. Keep it out of the wrong hands.

"Wil, huh?" Jackson almost sounded jealous.

"Wilber Messing," Anna explained.

"That's some gift. Boyfriend?"

"He's a little out of my acceptable age dating range. I think he's like seventy." Anna picked up the camera and studied the wooden body. "It has to be a defect in the camera. Old lenses, old mechanisms."

"There is one way to find out," Jackson said. "Let's go take some pictures and see what happens."

"Right now?"

"Why not? If you're feeling tired, I happen to know an excellent coffee shop. I'm sure I can convince the owner to open up after hours."

Anna looked at the print. Unsure why she felt the strong urge to say yes to his offer, she nodded. "Where should we go?"

"Main Street?" he suggested. "There is always a lot of history in these old towns. Or the lighthouse?"

"My aunt did say that Cornelius was going to show himself tonight. What better way to see if we can catch a ghost?" Anna smiled in excitement. "OK. Let's do it. I'll grab my equipment."

Chapter Nine

Jackson wasn't sure what made him suggest a ghost camera adventure as a date, but as he drove through town he didn't care what they were doing so long as he was able to spend more time in her company. He enjoyed being with her. Unfortunately, it became apparent rather quickly that she didn't realize it was an actual date. She treated it like a work assignment.

He couldn't get a solid read on Anna. She was independent and smart. That much was evident. She took care of her aunt, who by all appearances looked like she needed someone reining her in. The people in town had nice things to say about her, but no one pointed to a best friend or boyfriend. In that, she seemed lonely. She brought gift baskets to the hospital staff, donated food to the nursing home, and apparently the animal shelter. As they worked, he'd seen her leave food out for the stray cats in the back alleyway. There were also some customers who came in to pick up orders who had no record of paying. It didn't take an investigative journalist to realize she was discretely handing out free muffin boxes to some of the town's less fortunate. On the surface, Anna was too good to be true.

So, what lay beneath the surface? That's what Jackson couldn't figure out. He saw the secrets in her guarded expressions. His instincts told him there was more to her than he was seeing.

His instincts also had some other very baser suggestions it would like to make about his interactions with her. Damn, she was beautiful. No, more than that. She was exquisite.

First, they took a photo of downtown. The streetlights lit up the area milling with tourists. Cranberry Festival banners lined the sidewalks. Anna had pulled on a long sweater jacket to help protect against the chilly fall air. He almost wished she'd forgotten it, so he'd have an excuse to act like a gentleman and slip his black leather jacket over her shoulders.

Next, they drove toward the docks, to the road that ran close to the lighthouse. The moon was positioned in their favor outlining the dark lighthouse and distant cliff. Jackson waited patiently as Anna worked. Each photograph was a long process, unlike the quick snap of a digital camera, plus the camera itself needed time to be set up.

"Am I wrong, or are there a lot of cats in the area?" Jackson observed. The camera required longer exposure times to work, and they had to wait while it exposed the image to the photographic paper. Cats kept running through the frame and would surely show up as blurs later.

Moonlight caressed Anna's face as she turned toward him. The soft blue caught in her eyes, making them glimmer with an almost magical quality. "You don't like talking about yourself, do you?"

Jackson shrugged, trying to pretend he didn't know what she was talking about. He'd been evading her personal questions all day. "I do talk about myself."

"No, you avoid my questions with more questions. I ask you how old you were when you last visited Everlasting, and you ask me about the history of photography. I ask if your parents are still in the area, and you try to distract me with the number of cats in—"

"Both of my parents have passed. My mother when I was younger, and we lived here, and my father a few years back. I don't like to talk about it." It wasn't a lie. He didn't like talking about his parents.

"I'm sorry you lost them." Anna touched his arm. His skin tingled at the contact. He stared at her hand.

"I was happy when we left this place, and I

didn't want to come back. It seemed strange at the time that my editor would tell me to write about the mysteries surrounding the Cranberry Festival in a small Northeastern seaside town. It's not like I ever talked about this place. When I agreed, I didn't think I'd find anything worth saying. I almost said no to the assignment, but I'm glad I didn't."

"Why? Did you find your true calling working behind the counter at a coffee shop?" Anna smiled. He loved it when she smiled. Normally, she appeared busy and overly serious, so that when she smiled at him, the look appeared genuine.

"I had fun today," he admitted.

"Why do you think your editor sent you to Everlasting?"

"You know how this place is. You know the supernatural happenings and things that can't be explained. I think he sent me for the same reason I couldn't turn it down. Something, or someone, wanted me to be here. They emailed my editor with strange tips and leads, suggesting I come to your coffee shop to hire a local photographer to show me around. And I think it has something to do with what happened to George. Every instinct I have tells me that there is a mystery here and I intend to solve it."

"You believe someone lured you here because they had a feeling that something bad was going to happen?" Anna shook her head in disbelief. "That makes no sense, Jackson. Why you? Why not go to the police?"

"You saw how incompetent Detective August is."

"I'll give you that." Anna covered the lens to stop the exposure. "We're done here. Where to next? Graveyard? There are bound to be ghosts there."

"You don't believe me, do you?"

"No, I believe you might have been compelled to come here. That's what worries me. There is only one person in town that I know who would meddle like that." Anna motioned that he should carry the camera for her.

"Who?"

"Polly." Anna opened the back door for him so he could put the equipment in the car. "She's been acting strangely, even for her. I'd bet she's up to something."

"She wants me to ask you out on a date." He tried to be charming, and usually, it would work, but Anna merely arched a brow. "Maybe all she is up to is playing matchmaker."

"My aunt carries a picture of me in her purse. She likes to show it to strangers during the festival and tell them I'm single. I once asked her to stop, and she said she was playing the odds. The more men she sent in my direction, the more likely it was that I would fall in love, have babies, and raise them to be…" She hesitated.

"Witches?" he added. "It's all right. I already told you, your secret is safe with me."

"What about your family? Any supernatural secrets?"

"Yes, I have my secrets." He nodded.

"You're not going to tell me, are you?"

"I like having a bit of mystery." Jackson shut the car door and leaned into her. "Keeps you interested."

"What makes you think I'm interested?" she asked.

"Call it a reporter's hunch." His eyes dipped to her mouth, and he leaned in to close the distance. He felt her breath against his lips. Her lids fell heavy over her eyes, and she did not protest his nearness.

"Anna! Thank the cranky stars it's you," Polly's voice interrupted from within the nearby shrubbery. "How did you get down here so fast? I just sent the mental message that I needed a ride and… Well, hello there, Mr. Argent."

"Cranky stars?" Jackson asked.

"Don't you see it?" Polly motioned to the sky, appearing from behind a nearby bush. "They're not happy about what they see. Something is amiss in the ocean tonight."

"I take it your date didn't go too well?" Anna asked. She met his eyes briefly before turning toward her aunt. "Oh, Polly, what are you wearing?"

"Rain suit." Polly wore a yellow rubber ducky rain slicker with matching pants and rain hat. Seconds later, bulging rain droplets the size of peas began falling on them. "And my date has been postponed. There were more important matters I needed to attend to this evening."

"Let's go," Jackson said. "Looks like a storm is coming."

"I'll drive," Polly announced.

"No," Anna denied. "You ride in the back."

Anna hurried around to the passenger side to get out of the rain. Jackson slid into the driver's seat and started the car. The headlights came on to reveal Polly twirling in the rain with a broad smile on her face.

Jackson looked at the woman's rain slicker covered in large pink polka dots. "Wasn't she wearing ducks a second ago?"

"Magic," Anna said.

"Really?" Jackson leaned closer.

"No." Anna laughed. "The material changes its pattern when it gets wet. For a reporter, you're kind of gullible."

"You seem to have that effect on me," he admitted.

Polly stopped twirling and ran toward the car to get out of the rain. The large droplets hit the top of the car harder but seemed to lighten as it fell through the headlights as if summoned to follow her. "The rain is vocal tonight. You two should have a listen."

"It's telling me to take you home," Anna said.

"Then you should pay attention." Polly hummed softly. "The universe speaks. All you have to do is listen."

"Witch's Brew?" Jackson asked.

"Garden Street, off Third," Anna directed.

"Number?" He knew where Third Street was.

"Oh, trust me, you won't miss it."

Polly sang softly in the back seat while tapping her fingers against the window in time with the rain. Anna didn't say much as they drove. He couldn't stop thinking of their almost kiss.

As he pulled off Third onto Garden Street, he saw that Anna was right. There was no missing Aunt Polly's house. The front lawn looked like a garden gnome sanctuary. Rock sculptures and natural landscaping gave the ceramic figures hiding spots. Small pools and birdbaths had tiny houses that looked suited to fairies. Twinkle lights wound through it all, small dots to mimic frozen fireflies. Vines blocked the view of the porch, but the bright pink of the Queen Anne style home was unmistakable. It wasn't unusual for such homes to have bold color schemes, but he had never seen one quite like this.

The weather had cleared on the drive over. The dry road and sidewalks indicated that rain had not fallen on this side of town. Jackson stepped out of the car to open Polly's door for her.

Somehow it seemed fitting that Anna's aunt lived in this wooden Victorian-era house. The asymmetrical three-story structure had a bright pink turret poking up on one corner over the top two stories that looked like the great-granddaughter of a medieval castle. Bay windows jutted out from the upper stories, accented by gables and dark roofing shingles. There were several applied features— brackets and roof cresting. Light pink and white accents curved around the roof, windows, and entries, and separated the levels like decorative lace icing on a cake. Jackson nodded thoughtfully to himself. That is exactly what the house looked like —a giant, crazy, pink cake.

Polly smiled at him and let him guide her from the car. She stood next to him on the sidewalk and looked at her home with pride. "I wanted sparkly pink shingles that would glitter like a disco ball to the heavens, but Mr. Cranky-pants Bob McGee said it wasn't possible. He said I'd blind small planes flying overhead. Some men lack imagination."

"There might be Federal laws regulating things like that," Jackson said, conversationally.

Polly arched a brow at him as if he were the

ridiculous one out of the two of them. "Come meet Herman."

"I—" He didn't have a chance to protest. Polly pulled at his arm to lead him through the lawn. He glanced down at the strange feel beneath his feet. If he wasn't mistaken, parts of her actual lawn might have been made of plastic.

He heard the car door open as Anna got out. "Polly?"

"Herman wants to meet your boyfriend," Polly said.

Jackson knew that the woman probably only called him that to tease her niece but he liked the sound of it.

"When I sent that spell, I knew you'd come home," Polly said.

"How so? You didn't know who I was until I told you." Jackson had to step over a mine field of gnomes. They looked like they were lined up to march against a tree.

"I didn't know this was your old home, but it is your new home," Polly explained.

"Polly?" Anna hurried after them. "What did you do?"

"You don't want to see it, Anna, but this one does. He's right about George. I read the cards so many times. I've listened to the signs. This can't be an accident. It definitely wasn't George's time, yet… his charts, his timeline, they're all wrong now. It sent a ripple through everyone's futures in town. Now I won't die with fire engine red hair, and I have to pick a new dress. Plus, the guest count is now uneven. Everything is swirled up."

"Dr. Magnus—" Anna tried to insist.

"Is a good man, but he's wrong this time. I know it just as I knew to send for you, Jackson." Polly let go of him and danced the rest of the way around the side of her house to the back yard. A small white, picket fence had been designed to enclose the area, but it was so low to the ground Jackson could've stepped over it. The landscaping featured a small pond lined with rocks and sand. "Follow your instincts, Anna. They're deep for a reason. So much is happening in town, just as the stars said they would. This is a strange festival year, is it not? And it's only going to get stranger."

"Funeral? Is she dying?" Jackson asked Anna under his breath.

Anna shook her head. "She's been planning that funeral party since I was a child."

"And you're invited," Polly told Jackson. "Wear a green suit."

"Green?" Jackson arched a brow. "Why green?"

"Because that will be the popular color that year. Bright lime green with banana yellow stripes." Polly motioned toward the pond. "Herman, I'd like you to meet Jackson. Jackson, this is Herman."

Jackson looked at the dark pond, not seeing a

lobster. Polly looked at him expectantly. He leaned toward Anna and whispered, "Is this a joke?"

"Polly doesn't joke about her Herman," Anna said. She looked like she might laugh at him.

"Is he invisible?" Jackson insisted.

"Oh, no, I'm sure he's in there," said Anna. "You're welcome to go for a swim and find him if you like."

"It's nice to meet you, Herman," Jackson greeted the crustacean. He had no intention of going into the dark water.

"Herman," Polly scolded. "Come out of there right now and say hello."

The water rippled a little in the shadowy yard lights as if the lobster was defiant, but Herman did not surface.

"Why are you such a naughty little boy?" Polly demanded of the water.

"It's OK," Jackson said. "We probably woke him up. It's late."

"You're a bad boy," Polly scolded. "No trip to Uncle Petey's for you."

Jackson swore he saw a head pop up but the moment was so brief, he might have imagined it. Most likely it was a play of the lights on the water.

Polly leaned over to pat a gnome's head before dancing her way to the back door. "Happy evening, children!"

"Night, Polly," Anna said.

"Good night, Polly." Jackson waited until the woman was safely inside her home before escorting Anna to the car.

"Did she actually say lime green and yellow stripes? I think your aunt wants me to dress up like a clown for her funeral," Jackson said.

"Probably." Anna chuckled.

Jackson wasn't ready for the evening to be over as he put the keys in the ignition. "Should we head to the next stop on our ghost tour?"

Hope filled him at the idea of being alone with her in some dark, secluded spot. Maybe they could finish that kiss they'd almost started. He looked at her hand in her lap, wishing it would fall in his direction so he'd have an excuse to hold it.

Handholding? Spooky dates? When had this happened? When had he turned into some nervous teenager on a first date?

"It's late, and I have to get up early tomorrow," Anna said. It was her polite way of asking him to take her home.

"I suppose the old graveyard you were telling me about will have to wait for another night." Jackson put the car into gear.

Anna stared out of the window. The streetlights danced along her features. After they had driven a few blocks, she asked, "What happens next with the George investigation? I'm not really the sleuthing type. I'm not sure what I can do to help."

"You believe me now?"

"I can't imagine anyone wanting to hurt George, but if you and my aunt are both so sure…" She let her words trail off with a sigh.

Jackson wasn't sure how he felt about Polly's tarot cards argument and talk of mystical alignments being the things that persuaded Anna, but he'd take the help any way he could get it.

"I've talked to most of the people who were there that night. So far nothing helpful, but you never know when all the pieces will fall into place and the puzzle is solved. I've gone through his social media profiles. Besides a rather manly obsession with posting about the different beers he's tried, there wasn't much besides selfies with various dates."

"Everyone knows George liked to date around," Anna said. "And everyone thinks of us as a New England fishing village. We have fishing, beer, and cranberries. I think several of the guys in town are playing that beer game. It hardly seems worth fighting over."

Jackson glanced at her more than he should have while driving. He couldn't help it. She was so captivating. "We should start by finishing the interviews of everyone who was at that party."

"We?" She finally turned to look at him.

"Ginger Madison won't talk to me. I think you'll have more luck since you know her."

"If Ginger knew anything, I'm sure she would be the first to hound the police to investigate the death. George was all she had." Anna again turned toward the window.

"All the more reason to try," he insisted. "I have some contacts who can look into George's finances to see if there's anything strange that shows up. I made a few calls and am waiting to hear back."

"That feels…questionable." Again, she turned to study him. "If it were me I don't think I'd want people looking into my life like that. It feels too invasive. We should let George have his privacy."

"I would," Jackson countered a little defensively. "If someone murdered me, you can bet I'd want no stone left unturned until justice was done."

Anna took a deep breath. "I apologize. I didn't mean to imply you were doing anything seedy. This investigation stuff is new to me. I'm used to minding my own business and taking care of myself."

Jackson drove under the speed limit, not wanting to drop her off at her home. Yet at the same time, he wasn't sure what to say. Generally, conversations flowed for him, but with her he found himself questioning his instincts. So, instead of an eloquent observation about Everlasting or witty prose to take her mind off her sadness, he ended up offering, "Polly sure does like garden gnomes, huh?"

"What?"

It wasn't poetry, but at least he'd drawn her from her thoughts.

"Oh, yeah. She thinks they're cute. Makes it easy to shop for her birthday." Anna leaned her head against the window and looked up at the sky.

"What are the stars telling you?" he asked.

"They are reminding me that I have to wake up early to bake cookies for they won't bake themselves." Anna gave a small laugh. "They're apparently not as insightful for me as they are with Polly."

Sooner than he would have liked, he pulled up in front of the coffee shop. "I'll carry the equipment inside for you."

"I can get it." She reached for the door handle.

Jackson placed a hand on her leg to stop her. The muscle stiffened beneath his fingers. "Allow me to end this date like a gentleman. I'll carry it for you."

"I, ah…" She nodded. He wondered if the firmness of his tone somehow stunned her into agreeing. Her eyes dipped down to where he held her leg. "Yes. Thank you."

Jackson stepped out of the car and moved to open the door for her. He offered her his hand. Her fingers slid against him. Every time she touched him, he felt a tiny spark, and each time the spark became stronger. Part of him wanted to run away from that feeling, from Everlasting, from what this place was and what that spark might mean. Sometimes he liked to tell himself that his childhood was normal, that supernaturals were just people, that Everlasting was not as mystical as his boyhood brain remembered.

It was easy to tell himself that when he was thousands of miles away, not standing in the middle of town.

Magic had made his mother insane. Spells and curses, potions and incantations, he recalled their fragments. They were symbols on the walls of his mind, and in the whispered echoes of an unwell woman.

"I'm sorry," Anna whispered, jerking her hand from him. "I didn't mean to."

"Mean to what?"

Anna moved past him and opened the rear passenger door. She took the camera from the back seat.

"Anna, what did you do?" Jackson didn't understand what was happening.

When she bumped the door with her hip to shut it, she forced a smile. "Now it's my turn to have a little mystery. Good night, Mr. Argent."

"Miss Crawford." He tilted his brow, wondering at the formal dismissal.

Jackson watched her until she disappeared into the building and then waited until he detected the lights of her apartment to turn on. He wanted to follow her. Closing his eyes out of habit, he projected his consciousness into the coffee shop. A soft light glowed from a few of the electrical appliances, and through the front window. Footsteps sounded overhead, and he knew she crossed to her darkroom. It was a quiet, intimate moment. He began to move toward the stairs, wanting to see her unguarded face. Did she feel anything close to what he was feeling?

Laughter rang over the street. The interruption was enough to pull him back into his body. A large group of twenty-somethings came stumbling in his direction. As one young man declared his love of cranberry brandy over cranberry vodka, it became evident that they'd been sampling liquors most of the evening.

Jackson glanced back at the window as he climbed into his rental car. He was a little angry at himself. Anna wasn't a suspect anymore. He had no right to invade her privacy. He needed to leave her be.

Chapter Ten

"I'm so-so-so sorry, Anna," Marcy apologized for the umpteenth time. Her short dark hair was pulled into two small pigtails that hung behind her ears. She had an excitable energy that the customers loved, one that became bubblier when fueled by coffee, and she was on her third cup for the day.

"Just don't let it happen again," Anna answered, as she had after every apology.

"Did I tell you how cute you look today?" Marcy continued, not trying to hide the fact she was kissing up to the boss. "I really like that shade of green on you."

Anna glanced down at the long sleeve t-shirt she wore. The apron covered most of the 1990s rock band logo on her chest. Sardonically, she drawled, "Yes, my jeans are a particularly nice pattern of distressed today, aren't they?"

Marcy laughed at the joke. "Did I say I was sorry for yesterday?"

"How about you stop apologizing and tell me what happened?" Anna suggested.

"I didn't know Donnie was going to surprise me like that. Every thought just flew out of my head, and I didn't think to call until it was after hours." Marcy paused, lifting her hand to show off her gold engagement ring. Tattoos of flowers and birds swirled up her arm. "Can you believe it?"

"I'm very happy for you," Anna answered. Yes, she was annoyed about the missed work shift, but love was love, and she could forgive Marcy for the infraction. The woman was taking classes from an online college program and needed the income.

"I just had a brilliant idea. Do you think we can have the wedding here?" Marcy asked.

Anna chuckled. "Here? Inside the coffee shop? Don't you want some place romantic like out by the lighthouse?"

"No, I want something unique, and this is where Donnie and I met." Marcy put a drink on the counter and called out, "Gremlin Crunch-monkey."

A young man with blond dreadlocks and a brightly knitted hat laughed as he shot up to grab his drink. They received about a dozen fake names a day during the festival. Marcy took it in stride. As Gremlin reached for his iced mocha cappuccino, Marcy said, "You do know that crunch-monkey means you like to eat with your mouth open like an animal. You should work on that."

Gremlin looked confused but grinned and nodded.

Marcy turned back to Anna. "Maybe we can do something with coffee beans in the decorations? Oh, or we can make a kind of Baby's Breath arrangement, but instead of white flowers, we'll glue coffee beans to a green craft wire. We could thread the tea bags through them like bigger flowers…" Marcy paused to read the next coffee order she needed to fulfill.

Anna laughed, only partially thinking the woman was joking. "What about burlap bag dresses? We can use the shipping bags the coffee beans come in."

"Yes." Marcy clapped her hands. "I love it! And we'll give out mini ground coffee bags as little party favors."

"I believe every couple's wedding should be what they want it to be, so yes, you may have it here if that's what you want." Anna leaned over to check the case. "I'll get more cookies."

"Take a break, boss. I can handle this crowd." Marcy pulled milk out of the small refrigerator and set it on the counter.

Anna went into the kitchen anyway. Upon entering, she jumped to see a figure looming against the counter. It took her a moment to realize who it was.

"I see you replaced me already." Jackson grinned. His blue hooded athletic jacket hung open at the zipper. He wore dark denim jeans and a fitted dark gray t-shirt.

Seeing him gave her a little thrill. The way her mind focused on him felt like one of her aunt's spells and the way her body tingled made her suspect magic was at play. Polly was always pushing Anna to fall in love and to have an adventure (*any* adventure). But falling in love because of a spell was not really love, and it wasn't the experience she wanted to have. It was magic, and magic could be like a drug, wonderful and powerful…at first. But like any addiction, it began to corrupt the mind with obsession, or jealousy, or in the case of her aunt, losing sanity in the form of hippie-like tendencies of dancing wildly in the moonlight and talking to inanimate gnomes.

All Anna wanted was a normal life—to work, to do good, to give back to the community, to not rely on magic.

"How did you get in here?" She glanced toward the back door, answering her own question. "How long have you been here?"

"Not long." He lifted a manila folder in the air for her to see. "I heard back from my contact. I think I have a viable lead in our case."

George. Of course, he wanted to talk about George. The pleasure she felt at seeing him did not lessen, but it did mix with a wave of grief over her lost friend.

"How did the pictures come out?" he inquired when she didn't speak.

"Why don't you come up and take a look at them?" Anna pulled the tie at her waist and slipped out of her apron. She laid it on the counter before leading the way to the stairs to her apartment. "Marcy, I'm taking a break."

"No, problem, boss—*whoa, hey*." Marcy stopped working as she eyed Jackson. "Hello there, handsome stranger."

"Hello," Jackson answered.

"So, you're heading upstairs?" Marcy wagged her brows knowingly at them. "To the apartment? Just the two of you?"

"Marcy," Anna gestured to the customers, "the counter."

"Got it, boss," Marcy replied with a laugh, before yelling, "Coffee wedding for two."

"What's a coffee wedding?" Jackson's steps hesitated behind her.

"Don't ask. Marcy's about twenty espresso shots deep into a caffeine buzz. She's not making any sense." Anna kept walking. She knew why Marcy was teasing them. Anna never brought people upstairs. Even though it was only a staircase away, being in her apartment felt like an oasis from work —well, besides the usual stack of receipts and order forms spilling over her small desk demanding attention.

She opened the door and glanced around to see in what condition she had left her home that morning. Her shirt from the night before was draped over the arm of the thick-cushioned couch. A pair of shoes were scattered where she had kicked them off on her way down the hall. Automatically, she reached to grab the shirt and sneakers before tossing them into the laundry basket in her bedroom.

When she came back into the living room, Jackson opened his folder and handed her a page. "This is his credit card statement."

"How did—?"

"Don't ask." He gave a small smile. "See anything strange?"

Anna sighed, swallowing her reservations about snooping. She glanced over the list of charges and frowned. "Yeah, George had a crappy diet and ate out way too much—taco trucks, burger joints, Chickadee's Diner, Frisiellos Italian food, pizza from Remos, Magic Eight Ball... Warrick's Surf & Turf is a clear favorite if the amount of these charges are any indication. There is at least two restaurant charges a day, except Sundays. Which would make sense. He would be at his mother's house for Sunday dinner. It's probably the only home-cooked meal he had each week."

"Guessing by the amount of many of these

charges, I think he bought dinner for two. Any idea who he was seeing? That woman with him at the banquet said they had just met."

Anna chuckled. "This is your new lead? I'm sorry, but I could have told you George was a hound dog. The better question would be, who didn't he date. I don't think there was one special lady in his life."

"Fair enough, but maybe one of them was jealous," Jackson surmised.

"Enough to kill? I don't see it. George didn't exactly keep his extracurricular habits a secret. Women knew what they were getting into." Anna flopped more than sat on her couch as she leaned her head back. It felt good to get off her feet if even for a moment.

"Jealous husband?"

Anna still couldn't see it. "George liked women, but he wasn't that big of a jerk." She studied the charges a little more carefully. "But this one, here, that's not a restaurant. Do you have any other months?"

Jackson handed over a few more statements. "What are you seeing?"

Anna scanned the pages. "Jackie's Carriage."

"That's not a restaurant?"

"No. It's a boutique baby store here in town. I've never had a reason to go, but I'm pretty sure it's just baby stuff." Anna frowned, as she flipped through the statements again. She found more charges for baby items. "There's nearly a thousand dollars' worth of purchases each month. Why would George be spending thousands at a baby store? And look at these payment amounts. He paid off his card in full each month. I doubt a delivery man makes that kind of cash."

"Depends on what he's delivering," Jackson contemplated.

"George can't be into anything illegal. That makes no sense. And I would have known if he had a baby." Anna flipped through the charges as if they would reveal answers. They only left her with more questions. "The only pregnant woman I know of is Dr. Magnus' wife, Cassandra, and I doubt George is buying them this many gifts."

"Baby items, a deliveryman, and unexplained income," Jackson frowned. "This doesn't look good when you add it all up."

Anna was inclined to agree that it was strange though she couldn't reconcile the George she knew with anything nefarious. "Lives are complicated. Maybe we're not meant to add the three things up. Maybe he had a secret trust fund, or got some kind of inheritance, or was lucky at cards. Maybe he donates to an orphanage."

She stared at the statements and didn't realize Jackson moved closer until he was sitting beside her on the couch. His hand touched her cheek, causing her to gasp in surprise and drop the statements onto her lap.

"I shouldn't have asked for your help on this," he said. "I'm sorry. I can see this is hard for you. The truth is often not what you want it to be."

"I'm glad you did. I want to know what happened," Anna leaned into his hand and closed her eyes. She waited for what surely would come next. When he didn't kiss her, she opened her eyes to study him. "What are you doing if you're not trying to kiss me?"

He gave a small laugh. "I was listening for Aunt Polly. That woman has horrible timing."

Anna pressed her mouth to his with a small moan. She'd been wondering what it would feel like to kiss him, and that desire had worked its way into her magic. His hand rested on her hip. The spark she felt between them intensified. Oh, but it was tempting. She could fall into that warm and cozy spell, pretend it was real.

What did you do, Polly? Not again. Not another spell.

Anna broke the kiss just when he would deepen it. "I'll get the pictures."

It took a few seconds before he released her hip. "Sure."

Anna went into her darkroom and momentarily forgot why she was in there. The feel of Jackson's mouth stayed with her. When she flipped the light switch, a red light flooded the room. The color of the bulb would keep the light-sensitive paper from becoming overexposed during the development process. It was sad that darkrooms were fast becoming obsolete due to digital media. The quiet sanctuary of black walls and the familiar smell of developer and unexposed film rolls always gave her a feeling of serenity.

She felt Jackson behind her before she heard him. Anna took a deep breath. She imagined tiny threads joined them, electrified nerve endings reaching out for a connection.

Logic warred with nature. The witch in her was tired of being denied. Magic tingled in her limbs, causing her fingertips to vibrate. Her toes curled inside her shoes. She felt the roots of her hair lifting. The intense reaction had to be a spell. That was the only thing that made sense.

She had to kiss him again.

Anna turned and grabbed where his face should have been. Her hand met with air. She frowned, having been sure he was right there with her. She swept her hands forward in the red light, even though she didn't see him. But she still felt him. "Jackson?"

At the sound of his name, he appeared in the doorway. He'd taken off his blue jacket. He didn't answer as he reached for her. Whatever this spell was, he had to feel it too. He kissed her as if he could think of doing nothing else.

Every reasonable thought left her. Moments passed with the blurring of her mind, and the dance of their fingers. The red light cast their bodies with an eerie glow. Her hip bumped a table. The small jolt shook her to reality, and she pulled her lips away.

"I'm sorry," she whispered. "I didn't mean to."

"Didn't mean to what?" he whispered back as if adhering to the quiet sanctity of the darkroom.

"Fall for the spell." She touched his cheek. The taste of him was on her lips. Her heart raced, and she felt dizzy as she tried to draw a deep breath.

"Well, I won't argue. When I kiss you, it does feel magical." He gave her one of his charming smiles, and she felt the pull toward him with a renewed force.

Her hand rested on his lower back, holding him to her as the hand on his face kept his mouth back. "Normally I can control the magic, but I might be due for a purge. It seems to seep out of me every time you're near."

"You call it magic, I call it chemistry." He leaned forward. "Who cares what the name is, so long as we both want it?"

"Spells aren't real," she countered. "They take away the will of a person. They…"

How could she explain?

His smile widened. "So, you're saying you

wanted me so badly you cast a spell on me to get me into your bed?"

"You're not in my bed," she corrected. "And, no, it had to have been my aunt. She can't help herself. She doesn't mean harm, but she's like a watchmaker trying to kick start my biological clock."

"A what?" He arched a brow.

"She wants me to have babies," Anna said. "More witches for the Crawford line."

At that, he leaned back. "You…want…a…?"

"Yes, Jackson," she drawled, "I want you to get me pregnant."

"Ah, well, I like children, but I don't think I'm in a place in my life to have—"

Her laugh cut him off. "Really?"

"You're joking," he stated as realization dawned on him.

"Are you sure you're a real reporter? You're so gullible."

"Only around you. There is something about you that I trust." He pulled her tighter against him and breathed deeply. "What if this feeling is just the way things are? What if there is no spell? How can you be sure?"

Anna wished what he said was true, but she couldn't trust her feelings. "Years ago, my aunt heard George ask me out on a date. I said no, even though it was evident I thought he was charming. She thought I was shy, and she cast a spell to encourage me to take a chance on the possibilities. The will was mine, the decisions mine, but my feelings were fueled by an amplifying spell that made me take the riskier path until I became lost on it. For five weeks, I thought I was in love. I thought about him, dreamed about him, became obsessed with hearing his voice. I made a fool of myself to anyone who would listen. He could do no wrong. George thought I was the perfect woman because I didn't pay attention to his flaws. I accepted his lack of ambition and made him cookies whenever he wanted. Ginger and Polly began planning our wedding. We looked at buying a house. It was ridiculous."

As she spoke, their bodies slowly pulled apart. Talking about Aunt Polly and her ex-boyfriend was a mood killer. Still, Jackson needed to know what he was getting into.

"How did the relationship end?" he asked.

"I noticed some of the rare herbs in Polly's pantry were running low. When I confronted her, she confessed to what she'd done. After I had stripped away the spell, I realized that even though a life with George was one possibility, it wasn't the one I wanted to take. He charmed his way through life. I work hard. He flirted with every female he crossed paths with and enjoyed stirring a little drama. I like to be low key." She sighed. Jackson had pulled away completely from her. She couldn't blame him. "I still care about him, but it wasn't love, not like it should have been. I think that realization hurt the most. I lost something I never had."

"And you think this is the same as that?" he questioned. The red light of the darkroom high-lighted parts of his face, but the cast of shadows buried his expression.

"You heard what my aunt said. She cast a spell to lure you here. If not for that, we'd not be having this conversation."

"If not for that, George's death wouldn't be investigated," he countered. "I have to believe things happen for a reason. Why does it matter how I came to be here? I'm here now."

Anna couldn't meet his direct gaze. "What about you? Have you ever been in love?"

"Once."

When he didn't elaborate, she finally looked him in the eye. "And?"

"Her name was Nicole. She was fun, made me laugh, and I thought it's what I wanted. But I really think I was more enamored with the idea of having someone that I ignored the obvious. She liked to make me jealous, as if it proved my feelings, and tried to get me to fight for her. After a fistfight one night, when some guy punched me and I was forced to defend myself, I realized the relationship wasn't what I wanted. I wasn't who I wanted to be. So, I ended it."

"What happened to the guy?"

"I broke his nose. It's nothing I'm proud of." Jackson sighed.

Losing love, even a falsely perceived love, had been hard for Anna. Losing her ability to trust her emotions as genuine, had been an even tougher lesson. His story said he might understand that. There was a reason most witches in her family line ended up alone.

"I'm a Crawford witch, Jackson. Our kind of magic comes at a cost," Anna said. "Polly should not have sent for you. She should have taken any suspicions she had to Sheriff Bull."

"Are you always so doom and gloom when it comes to relationships? What's wrong with seeing where this goes?"

"When it comes to witchcraft and relationships? Yes." She nodded without thought. Anna prided herself on seeing the positive in life, but in this one instance, it was hard. She had seen and heard too much over the years. "My great aunt Milly cast a powerful love spell in exchange for money she didn't need. The next day the love of her life had a heart attack. Milly was never the same at the loss of her Mr. Fuzzybutt."

"Mr. Fuzzybutt?" He gave her a bemused expression.

"Don't judge," Anna scolded. "She loved that bunny. She'd had that same familiar for nearly seventeen years. Great-great-great-grandma Amelia tried to end a war. She succeeded, but in exchange ended up cursing an entire village. I hear they're still afflicted to this day. You can't take from the universe without it taking something in return. And you can't throw something out without it giving something back. Life always rights itself. Everything must be in balance."

"What's the name of the village?"

"I can't remember," she said.

"Indisputable evidence," he teased. "A seventeen-year-old rabbit, and a no-name village."

"Laugh all you want. You've been warned." Anna scrunched her nose at him and turned to where she'd left the pictures to dry after she'd developed them the night before. She wouldn't risk standing in the darkroom with him much longer. If he kissed her again, she didn't think she'd be able to stop.

Anna took the photographs to the table and set them down. At first glance, they revealed nothing but a street scene with blurred people walking, and a lighthouse nightscape. A haze that could have been a moving cat smudged the bottom corner of the lighthouse scene like a furry apparition, but that was hardly a ghost.

Jackson leaned close to her. "I guess we should have tried the old graveyard first."

"At least I know it's not the camera." She leaned

over to study the print. "The ghosted image from the lodge photo is gone. Maybe it was a cloudy chemical bath. I was careful, but maybe I contaminated it somehow. It was my first time trying the process and…" Her words trailed off as she held the photo up to a lamp. Absently, she pointed at her desk. "Can you grab the lodge photo?"

"Here." Jackson handed her the picture from Diana Lodge of the Sacred Order of Hairy Old Men.

She placed it under the lamp. At his nearness, her attention stayed on his face. The smell of his cologne radiated with heat from his body. How was she expected to concentrate on what they were doing when he was so close?

"Is this the same picture?" he asked, not meeting her gaze.

It took a second for her to focus on what he'd said. She turned to look at the photograph. At first glance, the image appeared the same. The men's masked faces stared out like the meeting of a shape-shifter role-playing club. They stood in front of the lodge's stone fireplace, chests puffed out, their bold stances authoritative. Her gaze landed on George. His features were no longer blurry. He looked sad as he stared out at her, a sickly face trapped in dulled tones of yesteryear.

"He's not wearing a mask." Anna frowned. "That's not right. They were all wearing masks when I took the picture. I was so focused on the camera, I didn't even realize that was George under the wolf half-mask until he approached me afterward."

"The ghosted woman is gone," Jackson added. He was right. The woman's hip had disappeared. "I don't understand. Did you cast a spell over the picture to make it show us things?"

"No. I don't have that kind of power. At least, I don't think I do. I wouldn't even know how to begin such a spell." Anna went to examine the camera. It looked the same and gave her no clues as to what was happening. She set it down and then went to dig through the piles on her desk for Wil's note. Finding it, she held it up and read aloud, *"For Anna, I know you've had your eye on this. I haven't been able to sell it to you, for things like this should never be sold, but I must find it a new caretaker as it grows restless to be used. Keep it out of the wrong hands."* She gave the note to Jackson so he could see it for himself. "I thought Wil was being quirky when he wrote this, an old antiques guy waxing poetic about one of his favorite pieces, but there have been rumors that some of the items in his store are more than what they seem. This camera was kept in a locked case. Maybe the rumors are true. Maybe the camera is more than a camera. But then, I don't know why Wil would give it to me and not just leave it in the case where it was safe."

"In this town, I can't say I'm surprised there is a magical camera," said Jackson. "And he says it right here. He needs to find a caretaker for the camera."

"I'm a caretaker of a magical camera," Anna mimicked his words, stunned. "I'm not sure what this means."

"Why don't you ask Wil? He gave it to you. Surely he'll have answers."

"I tried going to his shop a couple of times to thank him for the gift, but he hasn't been there. His granddaughter was there helping to run the place. Penelope didn't seem to know anything about it, but she said she'd pass my message along."

"Wil must have thought you could interpret it if he gave it to you to use." Jackson picked up the lighthouse picture. "Does that look like a tentacle coming out of the water to you?"

"Maybe," Anna said, "or another chemical streak."

Whatever it was, it hadn't been there before. She glanced at the camera with an arched brow. What was it trying to tell her?

"I think we can agree that these markings are not chemical streaks but clues," said Jackson.

"Here, look at downtown." He slid the Main Street picture to the top of the stack. "Is that someone on fire beneath the banner? Am I wrong, or does that look like some kind of Salem witch trial thing happening?"

"Witch burning? There hasn't been a record of one of those in this town since the late 1600s." When he gave her a strange look, she explained, "I took some photographs for the local museum's brochures. They had a whole display on witch trials and superstitions. Terrifying stuff when that's your bloodline. Though, if I remember correctly most of the women persecuted by zealots weren't actually of witch blood. Witches didn't tend to get caught by humans like that. We had to look out for the hunters. They were the real threat. Still are."

"Why would the camera show you a four-hundred-year-old tragedy?" Jackson tapped his fingers as he contemplated the evidence before them.

"Maybe the witch died too young, like George? Maybe ghosts are trying to tell us some clue as to who is responsible for their deaths? How am I supposed to know?" Anna went to the kitchen to fetch two glasses of ice water. She took a long drink before handing the other glass to Jackson.

Jackson accepted the water. "If this camera is meant to be with you, then I have to think you're the one who can answer these questions. What do your instincts tell you when you look at them?"

"That I'm way out of my league," Anna admitted. "I don't actively practice magic."

"Take a deep breath and try to relax. What do you think the tentacle thing by the lighthouse could be? Just say what pops into your head when you look at it."

"I don't know. Perhaps a guy with a squid tattoo murdered a sailor sometime within the last three centuries?" Anna sighed in frustration. "What I do know is that I can't do anything about a crime from the nineteenth century, or a squid versus lighthouse science fiction movie, but this…" She lifted the photo of George. The mask was back over the man's face. The image on the picture never visibly moved, and the changes happened when they weren't looking. "This we can do something about. Let's go talk to Ginger. See if she knows anything about the strange credit card charges."

"What about the coffee shop?" Jackson asked. "Are you OK to leave work right now?"

"Marcy can handle it. She owes me one for missing work." Anna reached for her messenger bag style purse and slipped the thick strap over her head. Anna loved cute purses but didn't indulge in buying them like she wanted. The khaki colored material matched everything she owned. She draped a light hoodie over the body of her purse to carry it in case the fall breeze coming off the ocean suddenly turned chilly.

"Wait, Anna," Jackson stopped her from leaving. "Don't you think we should talk more about…?" His eyes moved toward the darkroom where they'd kissed.

"I thought we had," she said. "As much as I want to kiss you right now and forget everything else, I can't do it."

"Why?"

Anna liked Jackson. She didn't want to hurt him by allowing him to fall into a lie. There were times with George indicated he'd never recovered from their brief engagement, even though they'd managed to be friends. "I won't allow myself to fall in love with a spell again."

Chapter Eleven

Ginger Madison lived in a white shingle style home in an old neighborhood, the kind of area where people thought little of property value. Though nice, it didn't have the character of Polly's Queen Anne. Classical black columns accented a wrap-around porch. There was less detailing around the windows and doors than other houses built in the same time period, but it did have an irregular roof line with intersecting cross gables that made it visually appealing to look at. The first story was made of stone while shingles covering the second story. The most striking feature was the Palladian windows. At two stories, it towered slightly over its ranch style neighbors.

Houses along the street had been built sporadically over the decades so that a bright purple, grand Victorian sat next to a prefab two story box, next to a split-level ranch home, next to the Madison home. The yards were left in various states of care and neglect. Incomplete wooden fences lined a yard, not really keeping anything out or in. One family had a fake water well with a hanging bucket, surrounded by flowers. The house next to it had what looked to be some kind of car part poking out of a jungle of overgrown grass.

Jackson observed all these things like a writer preparing a story, making mental notes of his impressions for later. It was an old habit. Anna wasn't really talking as she stared at the photograph of George, waiting for it to give her another clue.

"Anything else happen?" he asked, more as a way to engage her in conversation.

"Not yet. I'm trying to figure out what it's telling me. George is sad, a woman's hip, unmasked face, masked face..." She sighed heavily. "I'm worried if I look away, I might miss a clue, but at the same time I'm making myself blurry-eyed by staring at it."

Jackson parked the car along the curb in front of the Madison house. He wanted to reach over and grab Anna's hand in his. All her talk about spells didn't frighten him. The memory of her kiss lingered, but it was more than desire that clouded his emotions. She captivated him, completely.

Jackson wanted to make her realize that the feelings he was developing for her weren't just a trick of the mind. He liked her, a lot. Maybe even more than that. It had been a long time since a woman occupied his thoughts. When he was with Nicole, he'd been convinced he loved her, but it had never been this overwhelming and intense. One thing was clear, Anna was not Nicole. When he first saw her, he remembered thinking she was a work-a-holic and worried that meant she'd put her job over all else. That wasn't the case at all. Anna was busy, yes, but she seemed to put everyone else first—her aunt, the animals at the shelter, people in town who needed a little extra help. And she did it all without bragging, and without complaint.

Jackson thought about Anna all the time. When he was with her, he wanted to be close to her. When he was away from her, he was trying to come up with reasons to see her. He wanted to know her, really know her, and he wanted her to know him.

"My father was a thief," Jackson blurted.

Her eyes darted up to him, not following his train of thought. "Excuse me?"

"That's my secret. My father, Bad Billy Argent, used his genetic abilities for petty thefts and had a reputation in town because of it. It was the only job I ever remember him having. After my mother died, he became sloppy and ran into some problems in town. That's why we left Everlasting because the cops were keeping an eye on him."

She studied his face, and he wished he could read her mind.

"When I was fifteen he tried to teach me the life, how to collect secrets, how to use them to my advantage," Jackson continued. "Then one night I learned the secrets of a journalist. He was our neighbor. I watched him at his keyboard, taking notes. The next night I went back. And the night after that. I witnessed firsthand how he formulated his ideas, and then develop them, and how he pieced stories together from the smallest clues. I heard him talking to sources on the phone. I started following him around. I had never seen someone like that, working so hard to learn the truth. It was then that I realized who I wanted to be. I didn't want to be a thief like my father, always taking and scamming. I wanted to unravel a mystery so I could put pieces of the puzzle together to find the truth. I wanted to make sure the bad guys didn't get away with their lies."

"What do you mean when you say you watched your neighbor? You put hidden cameras in his apartment?"

"Nothing so sophisticated." Jackson didn't know why he was telling her this, but the words kept flowing. "My father's side of the family has the ability to teleport their consciousness. Many call it astral projection. My family calls it spirit walking. Our bodies stay in one place, but our spirit separates, and we can move about freely—through walls, into locked buildings. We can hear and see everything, but we can't speak, and people don't know we're there. My father used it to watch people punch in security codes and bank passwords. I use it to get to the truth of a story."

He glanced out the window. A green covered object appeared down the block and began making its way toward them. It took him a moment to realize it was a man wearing a spandex body suit.

"Do you spirit walk around me?" Her voice was soft.

He nodded, not wanting to lie. "I have."

"At the coffee shop? The morning of the banquet Polly was talking nonsense about a Lookie Lou lurker in the front of the store." She observed his reaction. "That was you?"

"Yes. Your front door was locked, and I wanted a peek inside before I came in. I heard you talking on the phone."

"I was talking to George." Her smile was sad as she looked down at the photo. "He was picking on me, pretending he gave my cranberry shipment to his mother for this awful punch she makes. He knew how valuable that shipment is to my business. This festival makes my whole year possible. Without it, I'd have to close my doors and find another job."

"Is that the real reason you don't want to kiss me? Because you're thinking about him?" Jackson couldn't help the suspicion. It would make sense.

"Yes, I miss him, but I already told you I didn't love him, not like that."

"What the hell?" Jackson jerked up in the seat, startled. The green man strode closer. Shocked, Jackson realized the man wasn't wearing green spandex. He wasn't wearing anything but tiny swim-suit bottoms. The entire length of his gangly frame had been painted green from hairline to toes.

Anna turned in her seat to look at the sidewalk. She gasped and jumped back a little in her seat. The man stopped adjacent to the passenger-door and turned sharply toward the car. Her hand slid onto Jackson's knee as she leaned away from the window. The green man jerked strangely as he came closer. He tapped on the glass with the tip of his fingers, and then he pointed skyward, and yelled, "Meep!"

"Templeton, get away from them." Dr. Magnus ordered as he made his way down the sidewalk from Ginger's porch. "They're Earthlings. Now go home and assimilate."

"Meep," Templeton answered, sounding disap-pointed. He moved away from the car door and continued on his way.

Anna leaned against her window to watch the strange man depart. "Since when did Everlasting make the first contact with aliens?"

Jackson stepped out of the car, and acknowl-edged, "Hello, Dr. Magnus, good to see you again."

"You'll have to ignore Templeton. He's going through an extraterrestrial phase," the doctor dismissed. "He's convinced he's from another planet."

Anna was slower to get out of the car. She smiled at the doctor. "Hey, doc."

"Hello, my dear," Magnus answered. "I was just saying that Templeton is harmless. No need to call the police. Sad case really. The man is a bonafide genius. He developed a formula for rocket fuel before falling off the deep end. This month he's an alien. Last month he found an old army uniform, declared himself a general, and convinced some woman to push him around town in a shopping cart."

"Shouldn't someone do something to help him?" Anna asked.

"He's never harmed a soul, and his mother looks after him," Magnus dismissed her concern. "Are you here to check on Ginger? I'm sure she'll be glad to see you, Anna. I know she had high hopes for you and George getting together."

"Jackson, would you mind grabbing that box of muffins for me?" Anna cast a sidelong glance at Jackson.

"Sure." He went to get the box out of the backseat.

To Magnus, she asked, keeping her voice soft as

if Jackson wouldn't hear it, "What actually happened? Are you positive it was an accident?"

"Yes. He had an allergic reaction," the doctor asserted.

"I know that's the official story, but doc, the green foam that was coming out of his mouth. I've never heard of an allergic reaction that included—"

"Listen." Magnus put a hand on her arm. "I know it can be difficult to understand when we lose someone so young and healthy, but these things do happen. I looked into the case myself. He had a rare genetic, allergic reaction to some kind of silver compound."

Anna nodded. "If you say so."

"I do say so." Dr. Magnus leaned over to kiss Anna on the cheek. "Listen, be delicate with her. Ginger's been taking the death very hard, and understandably so. She's not exactly herself right now."

"Vodka?" Anna asked.

The doctor nodded.

"I have the muffins," Jackson said, knowing he had no reason to be jealous of the man saying good-bye, even if he did kiss Anna's cheek.

"You're a good girl, Anna. I'll let you go see to Ginger." Dr. Magnus started to cross the street while digging car keys out of his pocket.

"Hey, doc, one more thing," Anna called after him. Magnus paused in the middle of the quiet street. "Did George have any other family I might not know about? Siblings? Cousins? Nieces? Nephews?"

"The Madisons only had one son," Magnus answered.

"What about kids? Did George have…" Her words trailed off as if she were embarrassed to be asking such a thing. "Any chance he was a father?"

"Why do you ask?" Dr. Magnus took a few steps back toward them.

"No reason. I thought I saw him buying baby items at Jackie's Carriage a few months back. It struck me as odd at the time, but I never asked him about it."

"As far as I know it was just him and his mother. If he had a baby, it wasn't born in Everlasting, or the mother never listed him on the birth certificate. This is a small enough town, I'm sure I would have heard something about it."

"Oh, OK, thanks. I wanted to bring care packages around if there were other family members." Anna smiled. "Thanks, doc."

"Anytime, my dear." The man waved as he finally crossed the street and made his way into a parked sedan.

Jackson carried the box for her as they walked up the sidewalk toward the house. "Well done. We'll make an investigative reporter out of you yet."

"I didn't really find out anything," she denied.

"Even if the doc did know something, he probably couldn't tell me much due to patient confidentiality laws. Though, I think he was telling us the truth. Doc is a good man."

"We confirmed George was an only child with no known offspring, so no known reason to be in a baby store making significant purchases." Jackson waited as she knocked on the front door. "And we met an alien."

"There is that." Anna gave a short laugh. "I really hope Templeton's mothership gives him the uniform back."

Jackson nodded. "I'll meep-meep to that."

Chapter Twelve

Poor Ginger was drunk.

Anna couldn't say she blamed the woman. George had been his mother's whole world, and without him, she appeared an almost empty shell. Her pain was seen in the small sniffles when she breathed and in the trembling of her shoulders. It shone in her glassy eyes.

Anna sat next to Jackson on the pink and blue floral couch, waiting in silence for Ginger to speak. Ginger shifted in a matching pink and blue chair. Her glazed eyes stared into the glass as if the clear liquid would give her some relief.

A porcelain serving tray had been filled with sliced summer sausage, cheese, and crackers, and left on the wooden coffee table. By the hard, dry edges of the cheddar, the food looked as if it had been sitting out all day, and continued to remain untouched. Next to the platter was the unopened box of muffins Anna had brought.

Doilies were laid on the arms of the couch. Anna drew her finger along the crocheted edge, pulling it straight. Time stagnated within the sad dwelling, punctuated by the ticking of the old grandfather clock.

"I'm going to look around," Jackson whispered.

Anna frowned and gave a slight shake of her head. Now was not the time to snoop through the woman's house. Ginger would surely notice.

He closed his eyes and leaned his head back. She felt a strange sensation as if someone stood over them, but when she looked around, all she saw was the quiet living room. Jackson's eyes remained shut.

Spirit walking.

"Ginger?" Anna asked softly. "Have you eaten recently?"

Ginger blinked heavily before looking up at her. "Anna? When did you get here?"

Ginger had opened the door to let them in. The woman was worse off than Anna first thought. Standing, she crossed over to the chair and gently took the glass out of her hand.

"I brought your favorites," Anna said, setting down the glass and opening the box she brought. She broke a small piece off the cranberry-orange muffin. "Do you think you can eat a little bit for me?"

144

Ginger nodded. Anna slipped a piece of food into the woman's mouth and waited for her to swallow. When she tried to do a second bite, Ginger placed her hand on Anna's wrist and held it away.

"You were always my favorite," Ginger whispered. "You would have made such cute grandkids. He never did tell me why you postponed the wedding. I guess it was because he was still dating. You don't hate him for that, do you?"

"No," Anna shook her head. "I don't hate him."

Anna glanced at Jackson. His eyes were still closed.

"Your friend is asleep," Ginger closed her eyes as if a nap were a good idea. "You should get him a blanket."

"Ginger." Anna gave her a little shake. "Let's get you upstairs."

Ginger didn't protest as Anna helped her up. They ambled up the stairs, taking one unsteady step at a time as Ginger leaned against the thick oak rail. Red carpet ran up the center of the wooden stairway to keep their feet from slipping. The stairs were open on one side with a rail and blocked on the other side by a wall. A prism hung before a window, spreading rainbows over the walls and ceiling. Family portraits hung along the wall, a mixture of George's childhood and family ancestors.

"Anna?" Jackson called from below. "Where did you go?"

"Here," she answered. "Can you give me a hand?"

Jackson appeared behind her and rushed up the stairs. He lifted Ginger into his arms and carried her the rest of the way up. He moved as if he knew where he was going, walking straight toward Ginger's bedroom to lay her on the bed. She mumbled, but her slurred words were indiscernible.

"We're not going to get anything from her today." Anna pulled Ginger's shoes off and set them at the end of the bed. "We should leave her alone. We will only stir up more pain with our questions."

"I agree," Jackson said. He patted Ginger's head, and whispered, "Just rest now."

"Did you find anything on your spirit walk?" Anna doubted it. Ginger didn't really seem like the kind to have secrets. As a beautician, she was always talking and gossiping with anyone who would listen.

"You should see this." Jackson led the way out of the bedroom and crossed the hall. He tried the doorknob, but it was locked.

"Can you project in and unlock it?" Anna asked.

"Doesn't work like that. I'm not corporeal." He pulled out his wallet and took out a small metal tool. Kneeling, he set to work on the lock.

Anna heard the latch click. "Should I be worried you're so good at that?"

He stood and put the tool away. "All part of the

criminal training package I received. Comes in handy when I lock myself out of my hotel room."

"Don't most hotels use key cards? You can lock pick an electric lock?"

"No." He reached for the doorknob and this time it opened. "But I don't always stay in the fanciest of places." Jackson pushed the door and stepped inside. "What do you make of this?"

Pink and blue striped wallpaper lined a nursery. Five cribs had been set up along one wall. A large stroller had been constructed to push multiple babies. Diapers were piled next to a changing table, a combination of sizes. Baby powder and rash ointment were laid out neatly. All the items were new.

"Well?" Jackson asked.

"Is someone having quintuplets?" Anna pondered, unsure what to make of the room. "I guess we know where the baby items were going."

"There's more," Jackson stepped deeper into the room and pointed at a wall.

Anna followed his lead. Framed baby pictures lined an entire wall in matching blue and pink frames—blue for boys, pink for girls—in rows of five. The display looked unfinished as the bottom row was missing two pictures. Though bizarre, the collection of twenty-three baby pictures would have been fine but for one very notable thing. Most of the pictures had been taken with a telephoto lens from a great distance.

"It's an interesting decorating choice." Anna watched Jackson snap pictures of the room with his smart phone.

"I don't know what to make of it." Jackson slipped his phone into his pocket. "Why would someone have a secret baby room with no evidence they were expecting a child? None of my initial assumptions are good, but then, I realize I'm jaded. The journalist in me knows not to jump to conclusions no matter how peculiar a situation looks, but…"

"What conclusions?"

"I am trying to be as objective as possible. If someone was to say to us, I'm working on a story where an unmarried man without a steady girlfriend has set up a secret room for multiple babies that no one knew about but his mother, what would you think?"

"Black market trade?" Anna gasped, shaking her head. "No. There is no way Ginger and George would be involved with anything as horrible as that. I'm sure there is a reasonable explanation for all of this. Maybe Ginger wanted to take in foster kids since George wasn't giving her grandkids."

"Possibly," he allowed.

Anna pulled on Jackson's arm, leading him back to the hallway. "We shouldn't be in here." She pushed the lock button on the inside of the door and closed it.

"Do you think George got a woman pregnant, and that she's expecting quintuplets?" Jackson paused on their way past Ginger's room to check on her.

"I can't imagine Ginger keeping being a grandma a secret." Anna didn't know what to think. The woman laid on the bed exactly how they had left her. "I can't imagine Ginger keeping anything a secret."

Seeing a liquor bottle on the nightstand, Anna went to grab it. She tucked it under her arm.

"I saw two more bottles downstairs. I'll get them before we leave." Jackson lifted the comforter from the end of the bed to cover the woman up. As they made their way downstairs, someone was entering the front door.

"Ginger, I'm back!" Cathy Jacobs was Ginger's next-door neighbor. Anna had seen the two women running errands together in the past. The color of Cathy's short red hair could not be grown naturally, and she wore more makeup than any woman should.

"She's asleep," Anna said, coming down the stairs.

"Oh," Cathy held two skinny brown bags under her arms.

"Are you kidding me?" Anna scolded. She hurried the rest of the way down the stairs. The vodka bottle she carried sloshed loudly. "The last thing Ginger needs is more liquor."

"How do you know what Ginger needs?" Cathy's eyes were rimmed with red as if she'd been drinking and crying right along with her friend. Her words were slurred. "She lost her son, and Captain Tom broke up with her, and she lost her only child."

"Give me those." Anna didn't give the woman much of a choice. She took the bags from under her arm and confiscated the liquor.

Jackson took two more bottles out of the living room and joined them at the front door.

"But, she wanted…" Cathy protested.

"You can pick these up later at my coffee shop downtown," Anna instructed. "If you really want to help Ginger, she is upstairs sleeping. Stop drinking. Keep an eye on her and let her sleep. When she wakes up, she needs to eat something and drink water. Any more liquor and she's bound to have alcohol poisoning."

Cathy nodded. "I can do that."

"I brought cranberry muffins. They're her favorite. You're welcome to have some." Anna tried to give the woman a kind smile, but in truth she was annoyed. The last thing Ginger needed was help to drown her sorrows.

As they left the house, Anna glanced down the sidewalk to see if they were alone.

"Looking for Templeton?" asked Jackson.

Anna cradled the bottles in her arms. "Can you believe that woman?"

"People don't know how to help when someone is in that much pain. What can you say but I'm sorry? I'm sure Cathy meant well." Jackson opened his trunk and put the bottles inside.

"Was I too hard on Cathy?" Anna glanced back at the house, wondering if she should apologize.

"No. I think you needed to be firm. She was half drunk herself. You did well not leaving them alone with more liquor. They need to sober up."

When Anna climbed into the car, she noticed the green nose and chin print on the glass. She picked up George's photograph from where she'd left it on the center console. There was no change. "Where to next?"

Jackson thought about it for a moment as he started the car before checking the rearview and side mirrors. "I think it's time we checked in with Detective August."

Chapter Thirteen

Detective August grunted in annoyance as he looked at the two, "amateur sleuths wanting to play cop," and his disdain for them was obvious.

Jackson had seen the man's kind before—lazy, arrogant, and more concerned about kissing the right backside for career advancement than actually doing some work. In this case that work should have been solving a crime. But if it wasn't high profile enough to get his name in the paper, August clearly wasn't interested. This wasn't just any old crime, this was murder. Every instinct Jackson had was sure of it.

"Ya should stick to baking and comin' up with them word puzzles for your fancy magazines," August lectured, trying to dumb down the tone of his voice as if Jackson and Anna were too stupid to understand. Jackson was pretty sure the detective thought he was clever. "The case is closed. Ruled an accident if you weren't aware. It's shut. S-H-U-T." August spelled the word out slowly.

Jackson didn't consider himself a violent man, but he really felt like punching this guy in the mouth. He refrained.

"I'm not asking about George," Anna said just as slowly. "I'm asking if any other strange things are happening in town."

"Read the paper, better still look on the *inner-net*." August brushed them off. He dropped his mocking tone and waved his hand in dismissal. "I'm not your local reporter for the news."

"Fine," Jackson said. "Thank you for your time, Detective. I guess I'll just have to interview someone else for this article since it'll probably go national. Come on, Anna. Let's see if that February guy is free. He'll make a good above the fold photograph. His picture will track well with our readers."

"Now hold on a minute," August said. "What kind of strange things do you want to know about?"

Jackson pulled out his phone and pushed record. "You tell me."

"Do you mean the unusual deaths by the shore?" he asked. "Or the reports of thefts?"

"What about anything involving children? Any gone missing lately? Any women expecting an unusual number of babies?" Jackson lifted his phone closer to August's face.

August frowned. "Is this really about the anniversary of the troll rumors? Listen, the department has already addressed our stance on anything supernatural. The troll calls were a hoax by kids twenty years ago. There are no missing children reported this year. No alien births. No cults. Nothing. Here's something you can quote me on, you're wasting your time. Everlasting is just a normal town with normal small-town crimes." August motioned toward the station door. "Now, if that is all you want to talk about I'm going to have to ask you to leave. I have more important things to do—like real police work. None of this Nancy Drew, Scooby—"

"Hey, August, the sheriff needs you to take this," Judy, the station dispatcher, called from behind a desk. The woman lifted a piece of paper in the air and waved it. Jackson couldn't see the lady's face, but he recognized her voice from when she'd greeted them at the door. "Everyone else is tied up on other cases. We have several reports from tourists of a naked green man walking along Main Street handing out maps to his home planet. And he was apparently caught trying to take a nap in the back seat of someone's car. Can you go pick him up? Sounds like it might be Templeton needing a ride home again."

"Yeah," Jackson couldn't help his slightly mocking laugh. "Sounds like you have some real police work to do, Detective. We'll see ourselves out."

When they stepped out of the police station, Anna gave a frustrated sigh. "That man is obnoxious. Though I have to admit, the look on his face when he was told there was a naked alien downtown was priceless."

"I have to admit I'm relieved there aren't missing children in town. That's at least something." Jackson offered his arm to her and was glad when she slipped her hand onto him. The light touch sent a spark through him. In some ways, this woman was a bigger mystery than the one they were trying to unravel.

"It still doesn't explain the nursery. I can try to ask Ginger about it later, but right now she's too far gone in grief and vodka to be of much help. Even if she was coherent, I'm not sure she'd tell me the secret. I can't exactly divulge to her that we picked a lock in her house and went snooping either." Anna gave a helpless gesture. "I guess we stare at the photo and see what other clues it wants to tell us."

"Are you hungry?" Jackson asked. "I heard Chickadee's Diner is meant to have great pancakes and milkshakes."

"I should probably get back to the coffee shop so Marcy can take a break," Anna said. "You're welcome to raid the kitchen there if you want."

"Sounds like a date." Jackson leaned over her to open the car door.

"A date at my own coffee shop so I can work?" Anna chuckled before teasing, "You're such a romantic."

"You want romantic?" Jackson grinned as she sat down, taking any opening he'd give her. "Why didn't you say so, darlin'? Too easy. I can do romantic." He closed the door before she could answer.

Chapter Fourteen

Polly would not stop grinning. Happy people didn't make Anna nervous, but her aunt had a look that said she was up to something. That usually meant a headache for her niece.

The room in the back of the coffee shop where Anna had let her aunt set up Polly's Perfectly Magical Mystical Wondrous World of Wonders was really just a converted storage room. In the center was a round table with a crystal ball and tarot cards for personal readings. The table was covered with a shiny blue and gold cloth embroidered along the edges with the pattern of suns and moons.

Shelves lined the walls and were filled with magical wares her aunt had for sale. Some were kitschy like boxes of crystals and rocks that were attributed with different healing powers—some real, some slightly exaggerated, and some that

Polly had found on the shoreline that were too beautiful not to have. There were potion bottles and tarot card decks, books on how to cast spells and make everyday magic, herb jars, and amulets. Near the floor were toys and witch costumes for the children.

Anna picked up a green, wart-covered rubber nose and held it up. "You do realize that some witches find this offensive, don't you?"

"Ah, but the children love them," her aunt dismissed. She was especially festive in her red and yellow maxi dress. Her glasses matched the red while her shoes and large chunky plastic jewelry matched the yellow. "There is no greater magic than the happiness of an innocent child. Besides, if people think witches are warted and green, it makes it easier for us to hide in plain sight."

"I guess so," Anna dropped the rubber nose back into its bin.

"Have you come for my rent?" Polly stood in front of Anna and lifted her arms to the side. She tilted her head back and said in a somber tone, "I bless this place with prosperity and light. I bless my niece with goodness and life." When she finished, she lowered her arms and patted Anna on the arm. "There you go. Good for another month."

"Thanks," Anna answered. Blessings were harmless. Even if they did go astray, they rarely caused any real damage. "But I actually came to ask you about George. Have you received any more signs from the universe?"

"Ah, so you believe me now, do you?" Polly nodded knowingly. "What happened?"

Anna thought of telling her aunt about the camera's strange power but then thought better of it. Until she understood what it was, she didn't want Polly playing with it. "You seemed so sure and I'm taking you at your word."

"Hm, sure you are." Polly frowned. "I suppose it has nothing to do with a certain silvery white that's come into your life."

Anna arched a brow.

"Mr. Argent," her aunt said, beginning to dance around the small room. "As in the argent moon that comes each cycle to bless the sacred objects of—"

"Speaking of Mr. Argent," Anna interrupted. "What did you do? I know you cast some sort of spell. What is it?"

Polly waved a hand in dismissal. "I already told you. I cast a spell to get him here."

"What else?" Anna insisted.

"Why does there have to be anything else?" Polly avoided meeting her niece's inquisitive and somewhat nosy gaze as she pretended to straighten her display items.

Anna picked up a small brown, very ordinary stone. "Fifty dollars for this?"

"Hold it in your hand. It has a good vibration,"

her aunt explained as if it should have been obvious. "I think it tickles."

Anna held it in her hand but didn't feel anything.

"I'm joking. I just have it there to pique customer interest." Polly pointed at Anna. "See, it works, it made you interested. It also helps me separate the charlatans from the real. I would never actually rip someone off by accepting money for it. Though, I could argue that a piece of earth is worth more than coin."

"Fair point," Anna agreed. There were more important things than money.

"Now, this," her aunt held up a small figure of a raven carved out of black onyx. "This you should give to Jackson."

Anna took it a little reluctantly.

"I found it in Idaho, near the Washington border, at a crystal shop. It spoke to me, and I had to have it. Now I know why. It was meant for you to give to Jackson. Onyx amplifies focus and discipline as well as wisdom. Ravens are very smart, so this stone makes sense."

"I remember," Anna said, recalling her childhood lessons. "And the raven is a messenger."

"Like Jackson," Polly agreed. "He messages the truth. This will help."

"I'll be sure to give it to him for you," Anna said.

"No," her aunt denied quickly. "Give me a quarter."

Anna didn't argue as she reached into her apron for change. She handed a coin over.

"Now you purchased it, and the gift will come from you. Trust me. Birds don't fly in a 'V' for no reason."

"You're right." Anna put the raven in her apron pocket. "They position their wings and flap in unison to catch the updraft of the bird in front of them to conserve energy on long trips. When the leader becomes tired, the bird falls to the back and another moves to the front."

"I don't think that's right," Polly said.

"I'm pretty sure it is," stated Anna.

"I seem to recall they do it in respect to the sun so their wings don't melt." Polly patted Anna's arm. "But yours is a lovely fable."

"Sometimes it's tough to tell when you're joking." Anna kissed her aunt's cheek. "I love you, you know."

"To the moon and back," Polly answered, "around the world thrice and—"

"—off into eternity," they finished in unison like when Anna was young.

"The fear inside you is held in place by pain and loss. Breathe it out," Anna said.

"I have to get back to the counter. I didn't stop Aaron from selling his CDs the other day, and now

Marcy brought in her art prints for me to look at for consideration. A boss' job is never done." Anna patted the raven in her apron, wondering if Jackson would stop by again that day.

"Say yes," her aunt instructed. "There are never enough outlets for the creative."

"How about I look at the zombie unicorn collection before I make my judgment?" Anna chuckled. Though, she probably would say yes on a trial basis. It was possible the millennials flooding into town would like edgy postcards from Witch's Brew.

Chapter Fifteen

"Happy birthday," Anna said, sliding the onyx raven across the coffee shop table toward Jackson. The last of the customers had just left, and she was locked up for the night. Jackson had come in about a half hour before without saying much as he waited for her to finish. Every time he caught her attention on him, he'd give a small wave as if not to interrupt what she was doing.

Anna had been keenly aware of his presence. It was hard not to notice the handsome man sitting alone, reading a paperback. His relaxed fit jeans and light-weight gray sweater gave him an air of mystery. He looked comfortable, but professional, and definitely not like the other tourists who were coming into the shop that day. Aside from a couple of doctors in scrubs, most of the men had been the garden variety saggy jeans and sports team t-shirt sort. There were also a few costumes since Halloween was a few weeks away. Several of the kids had painted faces—tiger whiskers, giant butterflies, flowers, and a big brown blob that might have started out as a football. She couldn't blame the women who'd hovered near Jackson's table in an effort to garner his attention. It didn't work. He was more interested in his book than in them.

Jackson picked up the small bird. "It's not my birthday."

"Polly insisted I give it to you," she said.

"Then please thank her for me." He ran his finger along the tip of the raven's beak. "I've always had a fondness for crows."

"They're smart birds." Anna slid into the seat across from him. "What are you reading?"

He lifted the book and handed it to her. The cover was torn, so she had to flip to the title page.

"The Passion of the Sparrow's Mistress," Anna read. "A pirate's tale of seduction and love."

He chuckled.

Anna arched a brow. "Is this a romance novel?"

"It's a swashbuckling pirate adventure," he answered.

Anna flipped to a random page to read, "His eyes said all, as they burned with a passion only for her. And at that moment, she knew the full will of her heart. The organ beat wildly in her chest, and Francesca leaned forward—"

Jackson snatched it away from her. "Margaret Anderson at the hotel's front desk gave it to me. I asked if they had any magazines, and she said this was much better."

"Oh, yeah, *Margaret* made you read it," she said in mock disbelief. "Sure, she did."

"Don't think I didn't see your bookshelf upstairs," Jackson countered. "Those weren't all mystery and suspense novels."

"May I get you anything to eat?" Anna laughed as she tactfully changed the subject.

"Actually," he reached next to him and lifted a brown bag, "I brought you something."

"Oh?" She lifted a little in her chair to peek inside. "More romance novels from the 1980s?"

Jackson angled the bag away from her and arched a brow. "Wait for it."

Anna sat back and watched as he reached into the bag. He pulled out a cranberry-colored candle and placed it on the table. It appeared to be the homemade ones sold down the street. Next, he supplied a box of cranberry-filled chocolates from another local business. Finally, he took out a bottle of cranberry novelty wine.

"This is——" she began.

Jackson held up his finger, silently telling her to wait. He took a lighter out of his pocket and made a show of lighting the candle. "There."

"You look pretty proud of yourself," she observed.

"You wanted romantic." He gestured at the table as if he'd fulfilled some kind of list of requirements.

Anna laughed. She held up the bottle of novelty wine. "You clearly haven't tasted this."

"Aw, it can't be that bad." His expression fell.

Anna tucked the bottle under her arm, picked up the chocolates, and then the lit candle. "Turn off the lights?"

Jackson instantly went to the light switch. Darkness filled the shop, cut by the streetlight streaming in the front window. The light from the candle flame danced along the walls as she led the way upstairs. She didn't bother to turn on her overhead lights as she let the candle guide her. She set it and the other gifts on the table.

Jackson's steps sounded heavy as he hurried up the stairs behind her. "Do you want me to turn on the light?"

"No," she denied. The candlelight cast a soft glow on his chest while hiding his face in a shadow. "Did you know that candles have meaning?"

"I think I've heard that before, but I couldn't tell you want they mean."

"For example, a green candle could denote money or luck. Blue is ideal for healing. Purple is wisdom. White is truth." Anna reached for the red candle and held it up.

"And red?" His voice was quiet as he moved toward her.

On the street below a random tourist shouted, proclaiming her undying love for someone named Ralphy, only for it to be killed by the sound of a honking horn.

The candle revealed more of his face the closer he came. It flickered over his features, drawing attention to his lips. Anna had become very fond of those lips. She remembered the feel of them, the taste of his kiss, the brush of his breath, the texture of his mouth. Nothing seemed to matter outside the flame's cast.

"Red could mean courage," she whispered, "or energy."

"I want to kiss you again," he said as if it hadn't occurred to him not to reveal such a thing so bluntly.

"It can also mean love, or passion, or even lust," she explained. "If I didn't know better, I would think you were trying to cast a spell on me with this gift, Mr. Argent."

"Well…" He grinned. "Let me put your mind at ease. That's exactly what I'm trying to do. What is romance but a spell that weaves over the senses? Wine to relax the day. Chocolate to sweeten a kiss. And a red candle, apparently, to make my intentions clear. I like you, Anna, more than I probably should, given the discouragement you've shown me. I heard your warning about your aunt's spells and I don't care. I don't need a spell to tell me I'm attracted to you. I don't need a spell whispering in my ear to make me want to be here. Let me be very clear. I want to be here, in this room, looking at you through the candlelight more than I want anything else."

"Jackson, I…"

"I want to kiss you," Jackson inched closer, "and I'm confident you want to kiss me back. But, if I'm wrong, then tell me to go."

Anna wanted to do more than kiss him. Every fiber of her being pulled in his direction. She felt her natural guard melting away. It had to be a spell, but she was beginning not to care. The careful distance she had created around her life and work (and the restraint on her magic) disappeared.

She knew when his lips met hers she wasn't going to stop him this time. Magic escaped from deep inside. The stereo turned on without anyone touching the dial and flickered through channels before stopping on a slow R&B classic. Their kiss deepened. Every candle in her apartment lit in unison. He swept her around in his arms, turning her toward the couch. His hands roamed up her back. The windows opened as if by their own accord to let in a breeze. Her curtains snapped as the soft sounds of Main Street rose to mingle with the music.

Anna leaned back on the couch, pulling him with her. The cushions pressed against her back as she sunk into the comfortable depths. She heard the sound of his shoes being kicked off and she hooked her toes on the heels of her sneakers to do the same.

Their lips parted, and he gazed into her eyes as if asking her permission to continue. The desperate intensity in his expression said more than his words ever could. The raw need he felt was undeniable. The cooler breeze through the window blew her hair against her shoulders, tickling her skin. The candlelight reflected in his gaze and outlined his muscles. She nodded once, giving him approval to resume the kiss.

If this was a spell, it was a fantastic one. She felt connected to him, more so than she had with anyone. Her skin tingled with passion and magic.

"You fascinate me, Anna," he half whispered, half growled against her. Jackson's gaze locked on hers. They found perfection in that heated moment and afterward Jackson held her close as they rested on the couch, cuddled in each other's arms.

Seeing the onyx raven on the floor next to his jeans, she leaned over and held it up in the candle-light. Jackson adjusted his body, letting her head rest on his shoulder. She set the raven on his chest. "What's next, messenger?"

The question hung between them. Even she wasn't exactly sure what she was asking. What was next about the investigation? What was next about their whatever-this-was? What was next when they stood up from the couch?

Jackson picked up the raven and gently touched the beak to her nose. "We find the truth in everything."

"That's a tall order." She turned her head so that the raven beak slid off her nose and she could look at him. His cheek was close enough to kiss.

He laughed. "I felt like I needed to say something profound, and impressive."

"You're trying to impress me? Why?"

"Maybe. Are you fishing for compliments?"

"It's working I'm impressed," she whispered.

"You are unbelievable," he said, closing his eyes.

"We should get up." Anna pushed up from the couch. His hands lingered as if he didn't want to let her go.

"Oh, yeah, I suppose I should get going. I mean, you had a long work day and—"

"I meant the bed is more comfortable." She tilted her head that he should follow before walking to her bedroom.

Chapter Sixteen

"You told me about your father. What about your mother?"

Until those words, Jackson had been enjoying his morning in Anna's bed. There was a quiet perfection to watching the sunrise cast its orange glow over her naked back as the soft sounds of her breathing undulated in the air like a sweet melody.

He knew Anna didn't mean anything by her questions, and couldn't take offense, but it wasn't a subject he was used to talking about.

"What would you say to breakfast in bed?" Jackson pressed a light kiss to the corner of her mouth and sat up.

"That I'm low on groceries and you better not walk downstairs wearing that outfit." She gave him a once over and winked. "Let me take a quick shower, and I'll go downstairs to get us something."

She was closing the door to the shower before he could answer. He thought about joining her but instead found himself going to the living room to look for his boxers and t-shirt. As he passed the table, he saw the Sacred Order of Hairy Old Men banquet photograph. George faced sideways, and his hand was lifted as if holding an invisible object.

Jackson wasn't convinced the photograph was all that helpful. Its mysterious hints were more frustrating than anything. Hearing the shower still running, he went toward the camera bag. The photo of the lighthouse now had a light shining from the lantern room on top to illuminate a car on a nearby cliff. The one of downtown had a woman in a tattered 17th-century gown standing in the modern-day town.

Curiosity got the better of him as he took the camera out of its bag and examined it. Aside from it obviously being an antique, it didn't appear out of the ordinary. The only marking was a small insignia that was carved into the base. It looked something akin to a hieroglyph or alchemist symbol. He lifted his phone and took a picture of it, determined to research it later when he went back to his hotel room.

Jackson returned the camera to its bag and sat down to study the three mysterious photos. His eyes kept moving back to George, the only mystery out of the three he had a chance of solving. He knew how much the man had meant to Anna, and that made it somehow more personal for him. He wanted to unravel the mystery. He wanted to give her answers.

Jackson cared what Anna thought, and what she felt. In many ways that terrified him. He could feel the attachment forming inside of him. When she wasn't near him, he thought about her. When he had ordered a hamburger, he wondered if she liked burgers. When he had walked by the library, he wondered if she liked to read books or only used them as decoration.

Jackson didn't know if it was really magic, but Anna Crawford had definitely cast a womanly spell over him. He was smitten. No, it was more than that. He could envision falling in love with her. Maybe he already was?

"Jackson, did you hear me? Shower's free if you want to take one." Anna slipped a hand on his shoulder. The alluring smell of lavender soap surrounded him. She kissed his cheek before leaning over to look at the photo. "It changed again?"

Jackson lifted the picture to show it to her. "It looks like he's holding something, but it's not showing what it is."

"Gah, this is frustrating." Anna made a small noise of aggravation. She wore a fuzzy pink sweater and dark blue jeans. He brushed the backs of his fingers along her arm to feel the soft material. "It's like the camera wants us to obsess over this image, teasing with little clues that make no sense—a woman's hip, a mask, no mask, an empty hand. At least with the credit card statements you found and the baby pictures on the wall, we have real leads. Granted, they're peculiar leads, but they're something."

"I feel there is something about these photos we're missing," Jackson said. "We should watch his hand to see what appears."

Anna nodded. "Why don't you take a shower? I'm going to run down and make sure Marcy is all set to run the store, and then I'll find us breakfast. I'll keep an eye on the photo."

Jackson stood to go to the shower, but then stopped to kiss her gently. "I'm glad I met you, Anna."

She nodded. "Me too."

Chapter Seventeen

Anna watched Jackson move down the hall and then reached for the camera bag. The double zipper was pulled shut the wrong direction. She was particular in her photography habits. She carried her camera bags a certain way and shut them according to the swiftest, easiest route to retrieve her equipment. Life did not stop and wait for its picture to be taken. Sometimes she needed to move fast.

Anna heard the shower start and opened the bag. The camera faced the wrong direction. Jackson had been digging through her belongings.

She frowned. What was he looking for?

Anna glanced around her apartment to see if anything else was out of place. She had nothing to hide, but that didn't mean she liked her privacy invaded. The papers on her desk looked shuffled about. Had he snooped around? Or was it something more innocent like the windows being open the night before?

After a cursory glance around the apartment, she went back to the camera bag and closed it. Her attention fell on the pictures, studying all three of them. George still stood sideways, but his expression had changed into one of panic. He now held something in his hand. She pulled the photo closer. It was a small raven.

Anna gasped. Her eyes went to the couch where the onyx raven lay on top of Jackson's discarded jeans. It was the same bird.

Her heart began to pound in fear. What was this? Who was Jackson? Why was he here?

How well did she actually know him? A feeling? A spark? An animalistic attraction? What was she thinking? She knew better than to rely on a spell-like reaction to a man. This was Everlasting. The playing field wasn't exactly fair when it came to romance. Some shifters had pheromones. Witches cast spells. Elfin descendants like George were naturally charming.

She slowly backed toward the stairs leading out of her apartment. She had known George for years. Now his image was warning her about the onyx raven, the messenger, Jackson.

Anna ran down the stairs. The lights were turned on, and the smell of brewing coffee filled the air. Usually, the scent was comforting in its familiarity.

"Hey, boss," Marcy said mid-way through flipping the open sign. "Looks like you had a long night. Tourists park for the evening and not let you close up again? I cleaned up the pots, and I'll get the floor done before the crowd starts."

"I'll be…" she mumbled, unable to form the words as she pushed out of the door onto the sidewalk. Her bare feet against the cold concrete was a shock, but she didn't turn around.

She glanced back and forth along Main Street, not sure where to go. She again looked at George's image in the brighter sunlight. He still looked panicked, and the raven was bigger.

Jackson did it. She breathed harder, trying to fight the tears that filled her eyes. *Did I sleep with a killer?*

Anna took off toward the Hunted Treasures Antiques & Artifacts Shop. She needed answers. Wil Messing was the only way she could figure out what the camera was trying to tell her.

Her hands shook as she pushed on the door. She used her magic to unlock it so she could go inside. She hoped he was available this time. Otherwise, she'd have to track him down. "Wil? Are you here? Wilber?"

"Anna?" Wil appeared from behind a display table. His salt and pepper hair stuck up in several directions as if he'd been running his fingers through it. The man was in his seventies but hardly looked his age. He wore a tan V-neck sweater over a striped shirt and dark brown slacks. He reminded her of the sweet grandfather she'd never known. "What is it? What's happened?"

"I…love…killer…raven…picture…George," she tried to explain in a rush of mismatched words.

"Whoa, slow down." Wil lifted his weathered hand to pat her arm. "Take a breath. What's happened? Where are your shoes? Is it Polly?"

Anna shook her head.

"Is it George? I've wanted to tell you how sorry I am to hear about your friend. We all know how close you two were." Wil gestured that she should sit in an antique chair, even though the sign on it clearly read, "do not touch."

"Wil, why did you give me the camera?" Anna asked, her words still coming fast. "What did you mean when you said I was the new caretaker?"

He looked confused. "Is that what this is about? I know that you'll take good care of it. Things like that need to be guarded by the right person. You'll make sure it stays up and hidden."

"Hidden?" Anna frowned.

"Well, on display at least," Wil continued. "Safe and where it can't cause trouble. Did something strange happen? I know some objects like to move around when they're settling into a new place. I didn't think the camera would do that. Usually, it just flashes when it wants attention. You can ignore the flash, it's harmless. It should quiet down soon enough. Nothing ever goes where it shouldn't be. If it's bothersome, lock it up with a few spells and make it stop."

"Why would I put it on display? It's a beautiful piece of equipment. It still works," Anna said. "I thought you gave it to me to use."

At that Wil swayed a little on his feet. "I figured it picked you so it could be admired. I never thought it would... You used it? But how? It's so old..."

"I made my own paper and developed it in my darkroom." Anna lifted the pictures clutched in her hand. "It's showing me things, Wil." The word was hard to form, and she felt a little crazy, even for Everlasting. "I think it's showing me clues to solve murders."

"Murders? Are you sure?" Wil pulled the glasses that were resting on the top of his head to better see as he took one of the photos. His rosy cheeks heated more the longer he examined the image. "It looks like the lighthouse to me. Did you not take a picture of the lighthouse?"

"I did but..." Anna took a deep breath trying to calm her racing heart. "It had these tentacle things on it. At first, I thought maybe they were chemical streaks from the development process. Then the light was shining at a cliff." She leaned over the photo and pointed at the edge. "See, that light

181

wasn't there before. You couldn't even see the outline of the cliff it was so dark that night. And there, that little image of a car, that car wasn't there before either. Also, Sapphire's cat is gone. It was a blurry blob in the bottom corner."

"What does any of this have to do with murders?" Wil asked, his gaze narrowing.

"I don't know." Anna looked at the other two photos and handed him the one of downtown. She couldn't bring herself to tell him about Jackson. "I took this on Main Street. It looked like a witch was being burned at the stake right under where the banner is. If I had to venture a guess, I'd say it appeared to be around the 1600s, and there was a woman in the crowd in a tattered dress, but they're gone now. I swear it was there. I'm not crazy, Wil."

"Please, sit down," he urged.

Anna listened this time. Her entire body shook. The photo of George seemed to sting her hands.

"I never expected you to use the camera," Wil said. He ran a hand through his unruly hair. "I suppose it makes sense that it would want you to be the one to use it, but still. I hadn't planned on that. I figured it was so old no one would bother to do anything but look at it."

"Then why did you give it to me?"

"I'm not a spring chicken anymore. I'm not going to be around forever. Penelope will someday inherit the store as is her birthright, and before that happens, I need to make sure that certain items go to the right people. She can care for most of them, she is a Messing after all, but some things can't stay in the family line. They need to transfer ownership, or they get restless and cause trouble."

"Does Penelope know she's getting the store?"

Wil gave a sheepish laugh. "I'm working on that."

"Wil, I don't mean to sound ungrateful with my questions, but I have to know what I'm dealing with. Where did the camera come from?" Anna persisted, almost scared to hear the answer.

"Sometimes cursed objects just become." Wil probably thought he was making sense, but Anna needed to know more.

"Become what?"

"Cursed, for lack of a better description." Wil rubbed the bridge of his nose under his glasses as if carefully considering his words. She imagined he had a lot of secrets and it would be hard for him to reveal them to her. "Sometimes items just become cursed or enchanted. As I've told Penelope since she was little, we Messings are the caretakers of the past, the present, and the future. We do what the universe bids." He sighed and seemed lost in his own thoughts for a moment. "Objects absorb energy or magic. Emotions imprint on places and things."

"So, what absorbed into this camera? Death?"

"I think a burning, deep desire," Wil said.

Anna thought of Jackson naked in her apartment and blushed.

"Not that kind of desire, dear." Wil sounded very grandfatherly as he cleared his throat. "The owner who had it before me said her father used it to play the stock market. Mr. Benjamin Harken desired riches and power. He had made a lot of money before the market crashed in 1929." Wil gave her a very stern look. "Now it's my turn to ask, what are you up to, Anna? Are you investigating the murders out by the cliffs? The ones that Deputy March had his eye on my granddaughter for?"

Anna shook her head. A customer had mentioned there being drownings along the shoreline, but she hadn't heard much about it. "No. I'm looking into George's death. I know they said it was an accident, that he had an allergic reaction, but I have my doubts. I can't explain it."

"You don't have to explain it. You're a Crawford. If you say you have doubts, I take you at your word."

"I'm sorry to hear about Penelope's troubles with Deputy March. Let me know if there is anything I can do to help her." Anna gave him an encouraging smile. "I don't believe she could hurt anyone. I'm sure the truth will come out."

"I think everyone knows Penelope didn't have anything to do with those murders, and Deputy

March and I came to an understanding of sorts. He knows what actually went on and I know he's got a thing for the Home Shopping Network. Now, if I could just figure out a way to get rid of Hugh Lupine..." He winked. "Just kidding. Kind of." Wil held up the picture of the lighthouse. "You might want to destroy this one since its story is told. Otherwise, it might try to make up new things for attention."

Anna nodded. "Yes. Thank you. If you are sure that it is done, and no longer needed. Take it. Destroy it. It will be one less mystery to torment me."

Wil went to grab an antique lighter from behind the counter and flicked it a couple of times until a fire burned. He lit the edge of the photo and waited for it to flame before dropping it on a metal tray. The image flashed like a camera strobe several times as if protesting. When it stopped, he stamped out the flames with the base of a metal cat figurine and then pushed the charred mess aside. "There, all taken care of. That won't be bothering you again."

Anna lifted up the picture from the lodge. "This is what the camera showed me this morning. George holding the raven."

"Interesting," Wil said.

That was it? Interesting?

"I'm not sure what it means," Wil said at length.

"The photo doesn't speak to my desires, so I'm not the one to translate it."

"I know who…" Anna felt a tear slip down her cheek. "I know who the raven is. I think George is trying to tell me who killed him."

Wil handed the photo back. "I wish you had never used that thing."

"What do I do?" Anna trembled. "I can't go to the police with a photo and crazy story. Even if they believe me, they can't use this as evidence. It would probably change before I even got there to show it to them. Detective August closed the case five seconds into it."

"Are you sure the camera is telling you the truth?" He went to the counter to grab a tissue box and brought it to her. "Maybe this is your 1929 stock market crash."

"What do you mean?" Anna frowned.

"I told you, these objects are cursed. Inherently they can't be trusted. It lures you in and then tricks you into believing something detrimental. Mr. Harken lost everything in one day—his money, his home, and a week later his life when unsavory characters came to collect a debt. He became obsessed with the camera, and it led him to lose everything. Maybe this raven that you're so upset about is your crash. Perhaps if you believe the raven, you'll lose everything."

A tentative hope filled her. "But what if it's not?"

"That's the thing. You never know. And maybe you lose everything if you don't listen."

"What about the witch?" She held up the downtown photo. "There is nothing I can do about a murder from the seventeenth century."

"I think part of you must be trying to connect to your witch past. It's no secret you don't…" Wil made a weak noise and cleared his throat. "That you're not like your aunt."

"Polly says I'm a witch in denial."

"I've known you a long time Anna. You've always been a good girl, coming by to check on an old man like me. I know you've been torn when it comes to your past. Losing both parents couldn't have been easy. You don't have to be like your Aunt Polly to practice your natural gifts."

"You started down this path, and you'll need to see it through. Use what the camera reveals, but use it wisely. Tread easy, Anna. I would hate to see you hurt." He looked as if he wanted to say more, but held back. "I'm sorry I gave the camera to you. I never meant to hurt you. I thought I was making the right decision. I was sure you were the person it was intended to go to."

"It's ok, Wil. I promise I'll be fine." She pushed up from the chair, feeling calmer than when she walked in. The mere idea that Jackson could be involved with George's death still worried her, but she became all the more determined to find out the truth. "I think I needed to talk to someone reasonable. Could you imagine Polly learning about a mystical camera? She'd enchant the thing and be down at the lighthouse trying to get a snapshot of ole Cornelius in his boxers. She's obsessed with that ghost revealing himself to her."

"You're one of the good ones, Anna," Wil patted her head. "Now go put on some shoes. This is not the weather to be running around barefoot." He paused, and a quizzical expression took over his features. He gestured toward the front door. "Does that young fellow belong to you?"

Anna stepped out from behind a display to see Jackson peeking into the window. A small tremor of apprehension worked its way over her as she met his gaze. She wasn't sure if it was because she was frightened by him, or because her feelings for him were just as strong as ever. "Yeah, that one's with me."

Chapter Eighteen

"What happened?" Jackson asked. He wore the some of the same clothes from the night before. He was missing his gray sweater, and the white under-shirt was slightly wrinkled from having been on the floor. "I thought you were going downstairs to get us coffee. Marcy said you ran out like you were being chased by killer bees."

"Marcy exaggerates," Anna dismissed.

"All right," he said as if unconvinced. He glanced down at her bare feet. "Do you regularly go jogging without shoes on a crisp fall morning?"

"Were you listening to my conversation?" she asked.

"In there?" Jackson pointed back at the antique shop. "No."

Anna wasn't sure she believed him. It was impossible to tell when his projected spirit was standing in the same room. She hated being suspicious.

"I tried," he admitted. "I think the antique shop has some kind of protection block on it. The magic wouldn't let me pass. I only ran into such a thing one other time, in a small Voodoo shop in New Orleans. No matter how hard I tried, I couldn't project myself into that tiny building."

She studied his face, unable to get the image of the onyx raven out of her head. George had appeared so panicked, so scared.

"Did something happen?" asked Jackson. "I feel like things are off between us. Did I do something to upset you this morning?"

"You went through my camera bag." It was a stupid reason, but she knew she was acting weird and didn't want to explain why. Anna wasn't ready to accuse him of being a murderer, especially in light of what Wil had told her about the camera misleading the facts.

"Yes, I did. I'm sorry. Should I have asked permission first? I wanted a closer look at the camera and the insignia on the bottom. I was searching for it on my phone trying to figure out what it stood for. I thought it might be a clue for us. I came down to show you what I found," he paused, taking out his phone to pull up a picture, "but you had left."

"You know what it is?"

"The closest I can find is this lunar glyph that means balance." He showed her a collection of drawings.

"It looks close," she agreed. "Not sure it helps."

"So, was that Wilber you were talking to? The antiques guy who gave the ghost camera to you? What did he say? Did he have any insight into what the photographs mean?"

"Not really. He's just a caretaker of objects. He never actually used the camera, and I'm not sure it's technically a ghost camera." Anna explained what Wil had told her about some cursed objects growing restless for new owners, and the camera showing the photographer hints of what they desired most. "I want to know the truth about a death, just like Mr. Harken wanted to make money. It must have shown him stocks to invest in, and now it shows George to me."

He studied her for a long moment. "There is more to it than that. You're not telling me everything."

"Apparently, it can also give false clues. So essentially, it's useless because it's too hard to say what is the truth and what is a lie. Then, when you consider that the clues are vague at best, it's more frustrating than helpful."

"That doesn't mean we can't look into what it shows us. Leads are never perfect, but it gives us a direction to look, doesn't it?" Jackson stopped walking and placed his hand on her arm. "Did it show you something else? Is that why you ran out of the coffee shop like you did?"

She didn't want to believe Jackson was an evil man. Everything in her told her he was good. But what if her feelings were because of a spell? Could she trust herself with him? She knew she didn't trust her aunt not to meddle in her love life.

"Please, just tell me," Jackson pleaded. "Is this because we slept together? Do you regret it? Are you embarrassed? Are you—"

"I knew what I was doing when I slept with you. I'm not some airhead who goes around doing things without thought and then later regrets it." Anna was not one to sleep around, and she didn't take the idea of a lover lightly.

"Good, because I don't regret it."

"Good." She nodded

"Fine."

"Fine," she repeated.

"Because I really like you, Anna." He stepped closer and cupped her cheek. "And I don't want whatever this is to be over."

"Well," she tried not to fall for the look on his face or the expression in his eyes. "I really like you, too."

"Good," he said.

"Fine," she answered.

"Perfect." Jackson leaned in to kiss her. Damn

him. How was she supposed to think when he touched her like that?

A passing tourist made a playful, "*whoo-hoo*," noise that interrupted their kiss before it blazed into something embarrassing.

Jackson pulled away and smiled at her. "Come on, let's find you some shoes. I'll let you buy me one of those orange-cranberry scones before I go back to my hotel room to change."

"You'll *let me*? Gee, that's so romantic of you," she said wryly. "Want me to buy you a cup of coffee too?"

"As long as it's not hazelnut," he said.

"You are so high maintenance," Anna teased. She motioned at him to walk with her down the sidewalk. The crisp air had a chill to it, and it felt like a rain storm was on its way. She glanced up at the sky. The sudden shift in weather felt like an omen.

"Can I see the pictures?" he asked.

She hesitated, wanting to trust him, wanting to feel the way she had that morning in his arms.

"Please?"

Anna handed him the remaining two. "I gave the picture of the lighthouse to Wil. He said that case was solved and burned the photo so it wouldn't cause me any more trouble. He seems to think the woman burned at the stake might be some kind of ancestor or connected to my heritage."

"How does that fit?" Jackson glanced briefly at the witch picture. All traces of the past had disappeared from it.

"Because I'm a witch-in-denial, as Polly calls it," she said, "and it is tapping into my innate desires to let the magic out."

"Why don't you?"

"My parents."

He waited for her to speak. When she didn't, he said, "Care to elaborate?"

Anna didn't like talking about it, but for some reason, she answered him. "My parents liked to renovate old buildings into affordable apartment housing. My mother was an architect, and my father was a contractor. We'd move to where the work was. There was an old building slated for demolition in South Boston. They were turned down several times when they requested the option to tour and buy, so my mother used her magic to prod the process along. She believed the neighborhood needed homes and a park more than another shopping complex. Plus, she loved saving the old buildings. This was one building they should have let die. It turns out the reason they were denied tours was because the structure was unsound. There was some political reason as to why the authorities didn't want the information public, something about a delicate police operation and shoddy contractors skipping corners. The building caved in during the tour. The realtor survived. My parents did not. Had she just done things normally, without magic, they would be here today."

"And you came to live with Polly," he concluded. "I'm very sorry that happened to you."

She nodded. The breeze became cooler and goose bumps lifted on her skin. She curled her toes. A storm was coming.

"Come on," Jackson led her by her arm. "You need to get inside. Your toes are red."

"Why won't you tell me about your mother?" She let him walk her back toward the shop.

"There is not much to tell," he said. "I was five years old when she died. I remember she was stunningly beautiful."

"But there is more to it, isn't there?" Anna had shared one of her most painful memories with him and hoped that he would be able to do the same. There was a strange relief in saying the words out loud, admitting to the loss, even though it was an old wound. She never talked about her parents with anyone but her aunt. "How did she die?"

"If I tell you, will you promise to go put on shoes?"

Anna nodded.

"My mother suffered from many things—a delicate nature, a troubled mind, a fanciful reality. I remember her playing with me for hours, spinning tales of knights and ladies. She became convinced goblins lived in the forest and were going to come and steal me. We stopped going outside. Every night, she'd huddle with me in my bed and whisper, *'Don't give in to the magic or the hunters will find us. They'll find the town and kill us all.'* I was terrified of the forest."

"Were there goblins?" Anna asked. It was a legitimate question considering the town.

"Maybe? It is Everlasting after all. Who knows what is lurking in the woods." He sighed shaking his head. "But I doubt it. She often saw things that weren't there. To a child, I thought it was like my imaginary friends and that we were playing. As an adult, I know she suffered from hallucinations and delusions."

"I'm sorry for your loss," she said.

Jackson cleared his throat as he took a close look at the more modern mystery before them. George stood like he had the evening she had taken the picture with a mask covering his features. The look of panic was gone. It was as if it had never been. Nothing appeared to be out of place.

"Ok, Mr. Investigative Journalist, what would you look for if we didn't have the picture?" Anna asked. Fact was, they both needed to change the subject from the distant past to now.

"I called Jackie's Carriage. Their voice mail said they were closed for remodeling and would be open again today. I thought we'd go there and see if she can tell us why George was shopping for baby supplies. Then I thought we'd try to talk to Ginger again and hope that she's sober."

Anna nodded in agreement. Both of those sounded like very logical courses of action. She wanted to know the truth about George. But the photograph had given her even more reason to find that truth—her suspicion over the onyx raven, and how it pointed toward Jackson.

"Now, shoes, you promised." Jackson looped his arm into hers.

"I'll go to the baby store on one condition," Anna said.

"I'm listening."

"You don't tell Polly we're going there." Anna gave a dramatic shiver. "That is one conversation I don't want churning in my aunt's brain. We'll come back to a list of possible baby names, magical self-cleaning diapers, and a surprise party announcing the news."

Jackson started to laugh.

"I'm not joking," Anna said. "My aunt loves babies."

"She'll never hear about it from me." Jackson swept her into his arms. She gave a small laugh of surprise at the sudden action. "You're walking too slow. Let's go find you those shoes."

Chapter Nineteen

If this was what Jackie's Carriage looked like remodeled, Anna was a little concerned about what it must have been like beforehand. Baby clothes were crammed into every possible inch on the clothing rack until the metal devices looked as if they might burst apart from the pressure. The clothes were organized into colors, not sizes, so chunks of pink, green, blue, and yellow created a pattern. Along the wall were baby carriages, car seats, baby swings, and other infant accessories.

Jackson led the way through the tight aisles toward where the cashier was set up in the back of the store. He'd gone back to the hotel to change into a fresh pair of jeans and a blue t-shirt. He wore a heavier jacket as the day was much cooler than it had been previously.

As a business owner, Anna wanted to fix the

glaring issues in the boutique. The register in the back would not deter shoplifters. Organizing by color didn't help the customer choose the sizes they needed. Also, there was something to be said for the saying less is more.

As someone who had no business telling Jackie how to run hers, Anna stayed quiet.

"Welcome!" a woman called waving her hand from behind the counter as if they'd have trouble finding her in the packed chaos of her store. Her bubbly excitement was as overwhelming as her decorating. She wore a sundress of baby pinks and blues, the style of which was clearly influenced by The Donna Reed Show. Even the short bob of her brunette hair seemed in line with the 1950s house-wife. "I'm Jackie Duncan-Owens, the owner, and I'd be tickled pink—*or blue*—to help you fulfill your baby needs today. We are very excited to present our new line of organic baby food, made fresh from locally sourced produce, as well as a line of all natural fiber baby clothing, which is so good for any baby. Your angels will surely notice a difference against their soft skin."

"Actually, we were wondering if we could ask you a few questions," Jackson said.

"Wait," Jackie held up her hands. "Here at Jackie's, we're family. I'm Jackie Duncan-Owens, and you are…?"

"Uh, Jackson Argent," Jackson's words sounded more like a question. "And this is Anna—"

"Oh, Jackson and Anna, how adorable!" Jackie exclaimed with a tiny clap. "Ha, Jackson and Jackie, we're practically twins. See, we're family already."

"We wanted to ask a few questions about—" Jackson tried to control the course of the investigative interview.

"I have to know," Jackie interrupted. "Pink or blue?"

"Uh, none," said Anna.

"I meant the baby. Do you know what you're having? Girl or boy? Pink or blue?" Jackie didn't lose her smile for one moment.

"Jackie," Anna said firmly, taking charge of the runaway conversation. The woman blinked, giving her full attention. "I'm Anna Crawford. I own Witch's Brew, the coffee shop and bakery downtown, and—"

"Oh, dear, no I don't drink coffee. Makes me too wired," Jackie interrupted, flinging her fingers erratically by her ears as of to signify going crazy. If this was what Jackie acted like without caffeine, Anna would hate to see the woman hyper. Jackie lowered her voice to a whisper while glancing at Anna's stomach, "And it's not safe for the baby."

Jackson cleared his throat, and Anna realized he was trying very hard not to laugh. "You know, dear, she's right. I've been telling you that for—"

"OK, Jackie, I'm going to need you to focus," Anna interrupted Jackson before he could spur the woman on more. "I'm not pregnant, we're not married, and we need to ask you a question."

"Oh, a baby shower?" Jackie tilted her head. "I have some lovely gift baskets."

"We're here about George Madison. I believe he'd been spending quite a bit of time here over the last few months," Anna said.

"Oh, yes, George. I was so sorry to hear about his passing. Such a tragedy. You can tell he's a very caring father. He only wants the best for his babies."

"So, George had children?" Jackson asked.

"Well, I'd assume so," Jackie laughed. "He's been ordering the top of the line everything for his two pinks and three blues."

"So, you've never seen the babies with him?" Jackson clarified.

"No, but he promised to bring me pictures," Jackie said. "Is that why you're here? You want to get his order? It came in last week. I wasn't sure what to do with it, as he prepaid, but if you want to sign for it…" She pointed behind her.

"Sure," Anna said. "We can take it over to his mother's house for you."

"Would you? That would be peachy keen!" Jackie went into a back room.

"Is it me, or is she like a crazy Donna Reed?" Jackson whispered.

"I thought that exact same thing," Anna agreed. "What are the odds that she's our guilty party? She seems insane enough to have—"

Jackie came from the back carrying five gift bags —two pink and three blue. Her demeanor had completely changed in the short time she'd been gone. She dropped the large bags on the counter. "I'm going to have to ask you to leave."

"Is everything…?" Anna asked in surprise.

"I'm not going to let you hurt my sister's feelings. She is an open and giving soul and what you said was not very nice." Jackie's sister looked exactly like her, down to every detail of her dress.

"Sister?" Jackson asked.

"I'm Janet Duncan. Jackie is my twin sister."

"We meant no disrespect." Anna hadn't thought their Donna Reed comment had been overheard.

"Maybe you should think about that before you talk about coffee in front of a pregnant woman. She's back there distraught," the twin scolded. She slid over a clipboard and pointed. "Sign here."

Anna quickly signed the form as Jackson lifted the five bags off the counter. "Please tell your sister congratulations on her pink or blue."

"Thank you!" a cheery voice called from the back room.

"I'll let her know," the grumpier twin said in dismissal. Her expression was tinged with an unreasonable anger.

Jackson led the way out of the store. When they were near the car, he said, "Keys are in my pocket. Can you pop the trunk?"

Anna reached into his jacket for the keys. As the trunk lid lifted, Jackson slid the bags into the back before closing it. She waited in the passenger seat for him to join her. When he closed the door, she said, "I'm changing my vote. I think if either of them is guilty, it's Janet."

"Yeah," Jackson agreed as he turned the key in the ignition for the car to start. "Who knew Donna Reed had an evil twin?"

"Did you look inside the bags? Any clues?" Anna asked. "Like monogrammed baby names? Customized ornaments? Something to indicate who the parents are?"

"I like your thought process. You're turning into a regular super sleuth," Jackson said with a nod of approval. "I didn't see anything useful when I glanced inside. They had a bunch of random baby items like bottles and onesies with little elves and trees on them."

Anna sighed in frustration. "How can you do this kind of thing full time? It's like looking for a needle in a haystack, only you don't know that you're looking for a needle, and you don't know that it's in the haystack. I found absolutely nothing useful about what we just did."

"I wouldn't say that. I think it was beneficial," Jackson disagreed.

"Oh?"

"We now have an excuse to stop by Ginger's house and talk about the fact she's got supplies for five babies in her home. I can think of no better way to open up the conversation."

"Maybe there is no baby," Anna said. "Maybe George had a crush on Janet and was using the purchases as an excuse?"

"Why Janet and not her sister?"

"Because Jackie is married."

Jackson narrowed his eyes in concentration as he drove down a quiet residential street. "That might be one thing we didn't consider. Maybe George got a woman pregnant who was married? Or maybe he was sleeping with a married woman? Let's think about what we know. George liked the ladies."

"And women definitely liked George," Anna added. "We have evidence of baby items, but no babies."

"Who do we know who is pregnant?" Jackson asked.

"Besides Jackie who can't have coffee?"

"What about Dr. Magnus?" Jackson turned down a side street. Anna recognized Ginger's block. "He was quick to pronounce the death an accident by anaphylactic shock, and his wife is pregnant."

Anna began to shake her head but then she

stopped. She took a deep, shaky breath. "I hate this."

"What?"

"I hate suspecting everyone in my life of horrible things." She thought of the onyx raven. "I've known these people since I was a girl. There is no way Dr. Magnus could hurt George."

"Even if he was jealous? His wife is rather young." Jackson slowed the car to a crawl as he looked out the driver's side window. "Templeton's back."

Anna leaned forward to see what he was looking at. Templeton stood waist deep in a patch of decorative grass. His painted green body swayed like it was in the wind as he held his arms up. "I don't think we're supposed to see him. It looks like camouflage."

Jackson gave a thumbs-up signal, and she swore she saw Templeton smile.

"Dr. Magnus helps people." Anna brought the conversation back to the subject at hand as she pulled the magical photograph out of her purse. All the masked faces stared back at her but one. "I don't think it's him." She held up the photo. "The doctor is missing from the group. I don't believe we're supposed to be looking at him."

"Hmm." Jackson tapped the steering wheel thoughtfully as he pulled along the curb to park across the street from Ginger's house.

"Unless the photograph is tricking us and we're supposed to be looking at him." She made a small noise of frustration and dropped the photo on the center console. "If this were a book, I'd skip to the ending to see whodunit."

"I know this is frustrating, but I feel like we're getting closer," Jackson soothed.

Anna looked up at Ginger's white shingle style house. The grass was a little too long, and Ginger had not put out her yearly fall cranberry yard decorations. Anna made a mental note to pay one of the neighbor kids to go over and mow the grass for the woman.

"Who is that on the porch?" Jackson asked. "Peeping in the windows."

Anna leaned forward in her seat and turned her attention toward the porch. The woman shaded her eyes as she looked into one window and then another. It took a moment to place the tall blonde. "Isn't that, what's her name, Darla? She was George's date to the Sacred Order of Hairy Old Men's cranberry kick off. What is she doing here? She knew George for less than a day."

Jackson frowned. "You would think they'd known each other longer by the way she was carrying on."

"Let's see what she wants." Anna pushed opened the door, ready to confront the woman. Going to the funeral was one thing. Showing up at

Ginger's house like a stalker looking in the windows was another. Jackson popped the trunk and pulled out the baby bags.

"I know you're in there," Darla yelled, slapping her hand against the glass. Her baggy sweat-shirt exposed one shoulder as it slipped down her arm. The neckline had been cut wide. She wore a tank top and tight black leggings underneath and heeled boots. "Open the door, Ginger, now!"

Oh, no she didn't…

Anna jogged the rest of the way across the street and up the sidewalk to the porch. "Can I help you?"

Darla gave a small jolt of surprise as she turned around. "What are you doing here?"

"Visiting a friend," Anna answered in the same rude tone. "What are you doing here?"

"That's none of your business." Darla placed her hands on her hips.

"I'm making it my business when I see someone harassing a mother who just lost her son."

Darla gave a small, mocking laugh. "Funny you should word it like that." She turned and began beating her hand on the window frame. "Come on, Ginger, you can't hide forever. I know you're there."

"Listen, nut job, get off this porch," Anna ordered. "If Ginger is here, she obviously doesn't want to see you. Let a mother grieve."

Darla sneered. "What about my pain? I lost him, too! I was the last person he was with."

"What about it?" Anna mocked. "You knew him all of seven hours. I think you'll find a way to carry on."

"You heard the lady," said Jackson.

Darla's gaze went to the pink and blue baby gift bags Jackson held before she again met Anna's eyes.

"I think it's time you went back to your hotel room and sobered up," Jackson said. "Let me call you a taxi."

"I'm not drunk," Darla denied, angrily storming off the porch. As she passed, she muttered, "Call yourself a taxi."

"Can you believe the nerve of some people?" Anna asked.

The front door cracked open, and Ginger poked her head out from inside. "Is that crazy woman gone?"

"Yes," Anna said. "We chased her off."

"Oh, thank you," Ginger sighed in obvious relief. She opened the door. The woman wore a pink silk bathrobe over her pajamas even though it was past noon. "She's been out here shouting for the last thirty minutes."

"Why didn't you call the police?" Jackson asked.

"There was no reason to bother the police about this. They're always so busy this time of year." Ginger stepped aside to let them in. "I don't want to be a burden."

"You're not a burden." Anna gave the woman a hug.

Jackson placed the bags on the floor. "Jackie Duncan-Owens asked us to drop these off for you."

Ginger blinked and looked at the bags. "Oh, she did?" She tried to act surprised but hardly sounded convincing.

"Ginger, do you remember when we came by the other day?" Anna asked.

Ginger began to nod but then shook her head. "Everything is a blur. I'm sorry, I don't remember, but thank you for checking on me. It makes sense. I saw the muffins you left."

"I helped you to bed, and when we were upstairs, we saw you had a room set up." Anna tried to tread lightly, but she needed to start getting answers to these questions.

"The room?" Ginger glanced up toward the nursery. "What do you mean?"

"The baby room," Anna prompted, wanting to end the charade. When Ginger didn't speak, Anna looked at her hand and thought of the witch burning photograph. Maybe the universe was trying to tell her something. She felt magic tingle her fingers. Its lack of use made her hesitant, and she knew if she allowed it to slip from her fingers to influence Ginger, the power would be potent and hard to control. It would also be draining.

Anna touched Ginger's arm, letting magic seep

slowly into her. She concentrated on an incantation, willing the woman to reveal what she needed to know.

"You saw that?" Ginger trembled a little and took a step back, pulling away from Anna. She rubbed her arm where Anna's magic had entered her.

"What's going on, Ginger? Why do you have so many baby beds?" Anna asked bluntly, now that she was aided by her magic.

Ginger shook her head as she rubbed the magic spot harder. "I can't…"

Anna felt mildly guilty about using magic to extract information from the woman.

"Ginger, are you in trouble?" Jackson demanded.

"Why would I be in trouble?" She appeared confused. It looked like she hadn't slept very well. Her eyes became glassy as the magic took hold. "I didn't do anything wrong. George…" She took a deep breath as she said her son's name and tears came to her eyes.

"Was George getting you babies?" Jackson asked.

Anna tensed at the question. Ginger nodded.

"Why would you keep that a secret? I think everyone would be happy for you," Anna reached to touch the woman's arm, but she took another step back as if to avoid the magic.

"From where?" Jackson's tone softened.

"Um," Ginger closed her eyes as if trying to pull the memory from a hazy place in her mind, "Boston. Sugar Land, Texas. Concordia, Kansas. Hernando, Mississippi. Spokane..."

Anna shared a look with Jackson. He opened his mouth to speak, but Ginger continued talking.

"Eddies Corner, Montana. Coeur d'Alene, Idaho. Nashville. Orlando. Juneau, Alaska. Cleveland. Southern California. Baja Mexico. Twins in Las Vegas. Halifax in Nova Scotia. Bloemfontein in South Africa. Iowa City. Wellington, New Zealand."

When Ginger paused, Anna tried to say, "Wow, that's—"

"Um, someplace in Oregon along the coast where they filmed those movies with the children going on a treasure hunt, and the cop who taught kindergarten. Oh, Astoria." Ginger nodded. "Astoria, Oregon."

"Ginger," Anna interrupted. "How many children was George trying to get for you?"

A tear slid down her cheek. "Only twenty-three. Well, five at first, but there are twenty-three."

"Was George adopting?" Anna asked, not sure she liked where this conversation was going. Why would George be collecting children from all over the globe?

Ginger shook her head in denial. She rubbed her arm where Anna had touched her as if trying to force the magical confession to stop. Whispering, almost desperately, she said, "I'm not supposed to talk about it."

"Jackson…?" Anna slipped her hand over his. "Do you understand this?"

"It's bad luck to talk about it before it is official," Ginger said. "We weren't going to tell anyone until the right time."

"Ginger," Jackson's tone was authoritative as he asked, "Are you adopting these children?"

She thought for a moment before nodding. "I suppose now I'll have to. George isn't around to claim them, and they are my flesh and blood."

It took Anna a moment to comprehend what Ginger was telling them. "Are you saying…? George has twenty-three children?"

Ginger nodded. "That I know of. The private investigator we hired is still looking. I really hope he finds more."

Anna's eyes widened. "Are they all babies?"

"The oldest is turning ten," Ginger said. "His mother is from Australia. Beautiful girl."

"Are you saying George had children when we…?" Anna let go of Jackson's arm.

"I so wanted the two of you to have a baby, too," Ginger said. "It was too bad you never liked my special cranberry punch. They would have been heavenly to behold."

"Punch?" Anna repeated weakly.

"It's a modified family recipe from the old country," Ginger said. Her words flowed more freely now as the magic rooted itself inside her like a truth serum. "It promotes fertility in those wishing for a baby. The fact you didn't like it means you didn't wish for a child with my George. I kept hoping that would change every time you came to dinner, but alas."

Anna was too stunned to speak.

"Cassandra liked it. I love seeing her and Dr. Magnus so happy and in love." Ginger smiled and gave a small sigh.

"Did Darla like the punch?" Jackson asked. "Is that why she was here acting all crazy on your porch?"

"I don't think George gave her any," Ginger said. "I was going to that night, of course, but then..." She sniffed and dabbed at her eyes. "I think she really cared about my son. She must have. George had that effect on women."

Strangely, the confession explained a great deal and made complete sense.

"Was anyone upset about George getting them pregnant?" Jackson asked.

Ginger's expression seemed to respond, *Why would they be?*

"You said the women wanted babies," Anna reasoned. "So why would you think the children were coming here? Are the mothers moving in with you, too?"

"I've been keeping track of the little dears, sending money on George's behalf. Sadly, the twins lost their mother, and I'm afraid three others are not in the most optimal of situations. George was going to claim custody of them and bring them here, but I guess now I'll have to pursue my rights as their grandma." Ginger eyed Anna. "Are you sure you don't want to try the punch again? The two of you would make such beautiful—"

"We're good," Anna interrupted. "Thank you, Ginger."

A knock sounded on the door.

"I bet that's Cathy," Ginger said. "This is usually her time to stop by."

"We'll get out of here, then," Anna said. "Be sure to call if you need anything."

Ginger gave her a long hug, murmuring in her ear about how much she appreciated Anna's friendship with her son. The knock sounded a second time. Jackson opened the door, prompting Ginger to let go.

Cathy's eyes widened slightly when she saw Anna. She lifted her hands to show they were empty. "No liquor. I promise."

Anna nodded and politely said, "Good to see you again, Cathy."

Cathy grabbed her hand as she passed and

squeezed it. Anna found the gesture odd but thought maybe she was trying to say thank you for checking on her friend.

As they left, she heard Cathy say, "Sorry, I'm late, Gin. Templeton was in my bushes pretending to be a weed. I had to threaten to prune him to get him to leave."

Jackson walked beside her down the sidewalk. They paused so a car could drive past before crossing the street.

"I'm beginning to feel like the universe is trying to make me get pregnant," Anna said. "Or maybe it's just trying to figure out this mystery. Everything keeps coming back to babies."

"You don't want children?"

"Well, someday, when it's the right time," Anna waited as Jackson opened her car door for her. She noticed he did that whenever he had the opportunity to get to her door first. "What about you?"

"I'm like you, I think. The situation would have to be right—the right woman, the right time, the right place." When they were making their way back toward the coffee shop, he asked, "Can you imagine, twenty-three kids?"

"Ginger said that and all I could think was bullet dodged," Anna admitted. "I'm all right with a man having children, but if that spell would have made me go through with a wedding, I get the impression a wedding ring wouldn't have kept George from spreading the love."

"Didn't you say he was an elf of some kind?"

"Yeah, his family line has descended from a Nordic elf clan. He never talked about it much. I can't remember the exact name, but I'd looked it up once, and they were forest elves, known to be genetically blessed with good looks, charm, and being fertile. I took it to mean the Madisons were unique like the rest of us in Everlasting. I never thought that translated into he charmed women so that he could sow his seeds wherever they could be planted." Anna pointed to the right. "If you turn here, you'll avoid a lot of the tourist traffic."

Jackson followed her directions. "Though, this does help in our investigation. If George was trying to get custody that might mean someone didn't want to give it up. A grandmother would have a harder time in a custody battle than a biological father."

Now that Anna had used her magic, she felt the power of it stirring inside of her. Her mind tried to follow the flow of it as it moved through her veins. For the first time in a very long time, she hadn't resisted what it was trying to urge her to do.

"Anna?" Jackson asked. "What's wrong? You're pale."

"We need to find Polly," Anna said, shaking. Her

head felt light, and she was having a difficult time concentrating. "I think I need her help."

"Anna?" Jackson grabbed her arm and gave her a little shake. "Anna? What is it? Stay with me, honey, stay with me. Don't…"

Darkness swallowed up his words.

Chapter Twenty

Jackson paced the length of Anna's apartment as Polly lit candles around her niece. Anna had yet to wake up, and he had doubts about whether or not her aunt was the right person to help her.

"I don't like this. I'm calling the ambulance," Jackson stated. "You didn't see her. She was shaking in the car. I think she needs a doctor."

Polly lifted one of Anna's closed lids. "What were you doing before this happened? Start with this morning."

Jackson hesitated, not wanting to talk out of turn about his night with Anna.

"Oh, trust me," Polly laughed. "The entire town knows you spent the night here last night. You two didn't exactly hide that fact this morning. You came down all crumpled with wet hair, and the two or you were seen kissing on the street."

Jackson felt heat warm his cheeks. If he didn't know better, he'd say Polly's pointed look was making him blush. He cleared his throat and couldn't meet her gaze. "We had breakfast here. Then I ran to the hotel to change my clothes as Anna helped Marcy with the morning rush and start the baking for the day. Then we went to Jackie's Carriage to ask about—"

"So, you met Jackie and Janet, did you?" Polly lifted Anna's other eyelid and examined it. "I swear those two are opposite ends of the emotional spectrum."

"Do you think they did something to her?" Jackson asked.

"They're harmless. At worse, Janet would try to make you question your life choices, and Jackie would throw you a baby shower." Polly checked inside Anna's ear. "Then what?"

"Then we were at Ginger's house asking about George, and then we drove here." Jackson leaned over, trying to see what the woman was looking at.

"Did you see any chickens?" Polly lifted Anna's arm and then dropped it so that it landed on her stomach. Anna didn't indicate she felt it.

"No," Jackson answered. "We drove by a fried chicken fast food place."

"Did you see a parrot wearing a dress?" Polly continued her strange examination.

"Uh, no."

"Anything unusual?"

Jackson thought of Templeton. "A man painted green pretending to be a blade of grass."

"I said unusual," Polly insisted.

If Templeton wasn't considered unusual, then there was nothing that would fit the woman's criteria for that question. "Not that I can think of."

She examined Anna's nail beds. "Who did she touch?"

"Um, me?"

Polly turned and looked him up and down. She came close and sniffed him. "Nice cologne."

"Thanks?"

"It's not you. Who else?"

"Ginger. Ginger's neighbor, Cathy, maybe."

"What were you asking Ginger about?" Polly inquired.

"Does this matter?" Jackson again reached for his cell phone and fidgeted with it as he debated about calling an ambulance.

"I don't know, does it?"

"Something doesn't sit right with either of us when it comes to George," Jackson said. "We've been looking into his death."

"You think Ginger had something to do with it?" she concluded in surprise.

"No, but some strange facts weren't adding up." Jackson lightly touched Anna's hair and watched as her chest rose and fell with even breath.

"What facts?"

"It's hard to explain, but it ended up being that George has children."

Polly nodded. "I can see that. Ginger never said, but that makes sense with their lineage and all. Ginger was always sad she didn't have more kids herself. A fertility elf without kids is like a tree without leaves. Barren and sad. Also, explains why she doted on George as much as she did."

"Well, I think that's not an issue anymore. Turns out, Ginger has twenty-three grandkids."

"Only twenty-three?" Polly shook her head. "Poor woman. I know she had her heart set on fifty-two. At least it's better than one."

"Does this help you figure out what's wrong with Anna?" he asked.

"Oh, I know what's wrong with Anna." She waved a hand of dismissal.

"But…? Then why are you asking me about chickens?"

"You looked worried, and I thought you needed distracting." Polly laughed. "Anna let out some of her magic, and I've told her, if you try to deny part of yourself and then use it all willy-nilly it will come back and pinch you in the sunshine."

"Do you mean to say it will come back to pinch you where the sun don't shine?" Jackson asked.

"Underground?" Polly scratched her head.

"No, your backside. I think the saying is 'where the sun don't shine.'"

"Why would the sun not shine on my backside? I was naked in my yard just this morning, and it shone on it just fine."

Jackson did not need to know that. In fact, the turn this conversation had taken was making him uncomfortable, and he wanted to back out of it.

"Stop teasing him, Polly," Anna groaned as she blinked. "Oh, my head."

"I told you, either use it or don't, but you can't just *dibble-dabble* with the *bibble-babbles*."

"Anna?" Jackson knelt beside her. He studied her face, thankful to see her eyes open. "I was so worried. Are you all right? What happened?"

"Apparently, I *dibble-bibbled* with the *babble-dabbles*." Anna blinked heavily and held her head as he helped her sit on the couch.

"You sure did," Polly agreed as she disappeared into the kitchen.

"Are you having some kind of episode? I don't know what you mean by that gibberish." Jackson stroked back her dark hair. "You're talking like your aunt, and you're not making sense."

"I dabbled with witchcraft and used my magic to make Ginger speak to us. It was an ambitious task considering my magic is unpracticed." Anna gave him a weak smile. "I'm sorry if my passing out scared you. But, like you said, we finally got to the truth of the baby mystery. I was tired of not knowing."

"Drink this potion, it will steady your nerves." Polly carried a mug out of the kitchen and handed it to Anna.

Without question, Anna gulped it down. Two seconds later, she was coughing violently and pounding her chest. "What was that? It tastes like hard liquor."

"That's because it's gin," said Polly, "and a few special herbs."

Anna handed the mug back to her aunt. "You couldn't have put the herbs in water?"

"Yes, but you looked like you needed a drink." Polly shrugged.

"Where's my purse?" Anna glanced around.

"I probably left it in the car," Jackson said. He'd been so worried about taking care of her, he hadn't thought to grab it. "I'll go get it for you."

He hurried down the stairs, but his progress was slowed by the crowded coffee shop. Several people blocked the end of the stairwell. The shop hummed with activity and loud conversation. Several people had brought their laptops. Some sat with head-phones on while they watched videos on their computers. Others typed furiously as if they worked on the next great American novel. In the center of the room, a group of twenty-somethings sat. They made up most of the noise as they debated whether sleep paralysis was caused by alien attacks or demonic possessions. A round of their loud laughter caused several of the writers to glance up in irritation.

Marcy came from behind the counter to the twenty-somethings. "It's a disorder caused by interrupted REM sleep. Our brains paralyze us, so we don't try to move along with our dreams. Sleep paralysis is when you wake up, but your brain doesn't know to let you move. It's not demons. It's not aliens. It's science." She set down a tray. "Here's your order. Enjoy your warmed gooey caramel cinnamon cranberry nut muffins."

"Nah, I'm pretty sure it's demons," a young man said when Marcy left. The group laughed again as they helped themselves to the muffins.

Jackson waited for a woman with a child to move out of his way before finally making it outside. The autumn temperatures had dropped by several degrees. Music drifted over the Main Street crowd. Jackson made his way to the alley near Witch's Brew to where he'd parked his car. He'd been in such a hurry, he'd forgotten to lock the doors. Luckily, Anna's purse was still there.

He picked up the purse and the photograph she'd left on the center console. Putting the picture into the purse, he then used the door from the alley into the kitchen.

Marcy glanced up as he entered. She was

pulling a tray of cookies out of the oven and gestured with her head toward the ceiling to indicate Anna. "How is she?"

"Fine. Better," Jackson answered. Marcy had seen him carry Anna upstairs. "How are you? That's some crowd out there."

"It's freaking insane. These customers just came out of nowhere like coffee-starved locusts to devour everything we have. But, be sure to tell Anna I got it covered down here. I don't want her to worry," Marcy motioned toward the fridge. "Any chance you can stock the creamer bar? That'd be a huge help. I called Aaron. He said he could come in for a few hours."

Jackson nodded. He knew how much the business meant to Anna and had no problem lending a hand. He set her purse on the counter and grabbed supplies. After he stocked and gave the creamer bar a quick wipe, he refilled the coffee containers and food displays for Marcy. She smiled in his direction several times, grateful for the help. By the time Aaron arrived, a half hour had passed.

Jackson almost forgot to get Anna's purse from the kitchen before rushing up to see her. As he neared her door, the sound of voices stopped him.

"It was only a little spell," Polly defended. He leaned his ear against the door to listen.

"It's never *only* a little anything," Anna answered. "Do you remember when I first moved here, and that boy was mean to me? I told you about it, and you cast a spell to make people like me."

"No, it was to help you find friends. You were so sad, my sweet girl. I only wanted you to find someone to play with."

"But I never knew if those kids liked me because I was me, or because you made them like me with a spell," Anna explained.

"Of course, they liked you. Don't be silly," Polly dismissed. "What's not to like?"

"And George? You cast a spell that almost encouraged me to marry a man who could never be faithful, and who had more children than one person should be allowed to."

"I only want you to find love," Polly said, "and that all worked out. Your magic stopped you before it went too far with George. You had fun, for a time, didn't you? It got you out of the house and on a few dates. What's wrong with that?"

"And Jackson?" Anna's voice was so soft, he could barely hear her. "I don't think you understand what you did this time."

Jackson wanted to project himself inside so he could see her expression. Was she sad? Hopeful? Angry? He couldn't tell by her muffled voice. If not for Polly's ability to see him when he spirit walked, he'd have been standing in the apartment in a heartbeat.

227

"What did I do? Jackson needed to come here. George's timeline was not supposed to end. Everything that had to happen because of that disturbance is now happening." The sound of footsteps cut off Polly's words.

"Polly, I don't think you get it. That photo I was telling you about showed me something. George's image…"

"His what, sweetheart?" Polly asked.

Jackson pressed his ear closer, waiting for the answer.

"The photo is magical, but it can lie, or tell the truth, depending on its mood, I guess. It showed that George was terrified of something, of someone," Anna said.

"Who?"

"It showed me an onyx raven," Anna admitted.

"And you think that means Jackson had something to do with George's death?"

"Not like he caused it. But what if Jackson coming here changed the timeline? This is why you can't cast spells without thought. The chaos—"

"Anna, I love you, but I'm going to say something you may not want to hear." Polly's voice was unusually serious. "Magic did not kill your parents. A spell did not make you feel what you're feeling now. That is not how things work. If that camera is lying to you, then it is because you're letting it. You are a Crawford. Stop trying to deny yourself. Strap on your conical hat, grab a broomstick, pick a familiar, and start singing to the full moon. You're a witch, Anna. Act like it."

"Do you swear to me on your love for me?" Anna insisted. "You did not cast a spell to make me fall for Jackson, or him for me?"

Jackson held his breath, not wanting to miss a word.

"I cast a spell to get him here because all the signs said I needed to," Polly answered. "And the signs were right, like always. He knew from the beginning something was wrong with this whole George situation."

"Where is Jackson anyway?" Anna asked in exasperation. "He should be back by now."

"He's outside the door listening to us," Polly said matter-of-factly.

Jackson instantly pushed open the door and tried to cover the fact he'd been eavesdropping by saying, "Sorry, that took a while. I was helping Marcy stock the creamer bar. Business is booming tonight. She told me to tell you everything is under control. Aaron came in to help, and she can stay as late as it takes to get cleaned up."

Anna glanced at her aunt, and he wondered if she was embarrassed by anything they had been talking about. He pretended not to notice.

"Thank you for helping her," Anna said.

"No problem." Jackson handed the purse to

Anna. He was relieved to see her eyes had cleared, and she looked like she was feeling better.

Anna dug inside her purse and pulled out the photograph. She turned toward her aunt. "You want me to use my powers? Fine." She motioned toward the table. "Jackson, would you mind grabbing that camera bag and giving me a ride?"

"Do you want to go take more pictures?" he asked.

"Yes. It's time we went back to the Diana Lodge to find out what happened once and for all." Anna looked at Polly. "I need Great-great-aunt Hilda's amplification potion."

"I'm not sure that is a good idea, Anna," Polly said. "That's like jumping into the deep end of the pool for the first time without floaties. You might not drown, but chances are you will sink and flail around."

Anna shook her head. "Just do what I ask, Polly. I need that potion. It's time to solve this mystery once and for all."

Chapter Twenty-One

"I'm surprised your aunt didn't insist on coming with us," Jackson said as he held open the door to the Diana Lodge.

"I told her the signs from the universe indicated she shouldn't." Anna stepped into the building. "Mr. Denton is in the back room working on accounts. He said we can stay as long as we like."

A flickering orange light came from the fireplace, the only source of light in the front hall. It was different than during a banquet when people filled the rooms. The sound of fire punctured the silence. She knew ghosts didn't need low lighting and a spooky vibe to haunt a place, but the atmosphere made her feel like a spirit might walk by at any moment. A small chill worked down her spine. Her eyes turned toward where the restroom was hidden around a corner.

The purple vial of liquid was unnaturally cold in her hand. Now that she had it, she wasn't sure she wanted to use it. She had a feeling if she drank the liquid there would be no going back. It was hard enough to suppress her powers.

"Do you want me to set up the camera for you?" Jackson asked.

"Not yet. Let's see if this room can tell us anything first. Could you get out the anointed candles my aunt gave us and put them in a large circle on the floor? They'll protect us from any ghosts or demons we summon." Anna pulled the lodge photo out of her purse and set it on the ground where the men had stood. She clutched the purple vial with her hand, hoping she wouldn't have to use it.

"Anna." Jackson didn't move to do as she asked. Instead, he looked at her for a long moment as if there was much he needed to tell her.

"What is it?"

Jackson cupped her cheek. Firelight danced on his rugged features and cast a mystical light into his earnest eyes. "I need you to know I didn't hurt George. I had nothing to do with what happened to him. I heard what you said to Polly. I don't understand why you saw the onyx raven in the photo, and I wish you would have told me that is why you ran out this morning to the antique shop. I knew there was something more than you were saying, and I understand that you distrust me. But, I need you to know that I…"

"I didn't say anything because Wil warned me the photo could lie. Yes, it freaked me out for all of a minute, but I wasn't about to accuse you of murder when I didn't think you were a murderer." She gave him a nervous smile. "I'm sorry I didn't tell you what I saw."

"Anna, I…" He took a deep breath and nodded. When he looked at her like that, all tender and questioning, he took her breath away. "So, we're good?"

"Yes." She nodded. "But maybe you should wait in the car. Or come back for me later? I don't think you should be here. I don't know what is going to happen."

"There is no way in heaven, or Earth, or hell that I'm going to leave you here by yourself." Jackson gathered the candles she'd previously asked for and placed them around her in a large circle. He then leaned over with a lighter. He only managed to light one before Anna used her magic. The flames ignited one candle at a time, moving around her until they completed the full circle.

Jackson started to smile at her in encouragement when a weak echo sounded, "*Rawr!*"

Anna gasped and looked around the dimly lit room. She motioned at Jackson. "Get in the circle. It will protect us if I do something wrong." Playing with the afterlife (and ghosts) was a serious matter. One wrong word or intention and she would turn light magic into dark and summon something altogether demonic.

Anna felt the magic tingling her fingertips, bursting to be freed. Energy flowed through her, lifting her hair from her shoulders like a stiff breeze. The fireplace burned hotter and brighter. She really hoped she didn't botch this up.

"*Rawr!*" came another cry, a distant echo. There were other words, but they were mumbled and hard to hear.

"I call upon my ancestors, guide me in this," Anna whispered. "I call upon my magic, help me in this. I call upon myself, please don't screw this up."

"Is that really a spell?" Jackson whispered.

Anna gave a small shrug. "I'm out of practice."

"Do you need me to say anything?" Jackson asked.

Anna shook her head as she continued. "I call upon the spirits shown by the camera to reveal to us the truth."

There was a rumbling sound, like the hooves of horses stampeding in the distance, but it was short lived. She looked around, willing the truth to manifest.

Jackson placed his hand on her shoulder but instantly pulled back as her magic seeped into his hand. "Anna, I have something else to say. It's important. Or at least, I think it is. Yes, it is. I want to…"

As much as she wanted to have a conversation with him, she really needed to concentrate. She felt the magic trying to work, the universe and spirits trying to listen to her requests.

"*Hairy bite.*"

"What?" Anna arched a brow and looked fully at him before realizing he hadn't said the words. The gravelly voice was familiar, in a way, but she couldn't place it. To Jackson, she said, "Tell me later."

"But…" He nodded. "OK."

"I call upon the past to reveal to us the truth," Anna said. She let the magic flow out of her.

"*To our ancestors' start…*"

Anna looked toward her feet from where the sound came. The photograph was moving. She quickly knelt to watch it. Jackson joined her on the floor.

The image flickered like a slowly moving flip book, an inch at a time. Anna recognized Herbert London as he was that night, holding up his hand in fake claws as he teased her with his poem. Behind him, she saw George caught in mid-laughter.

"*Everlasting ago,*" Herbert's voice said, the words skipping like a scratched record. The image froze, and no longer moved.

"Show me," Anna insisted flicking the photo

back and forth a few times as if shaking it would make the image go faster. They waited in silence for a long time. When nothing more happened, Anna slowly placed the picture on the floor and turned to look at the purple vial.

"Are you sure?" Jackson asked as if reading her mind.

"I know the answer is close. It's right here." Anna reached for the vial and pulled off the cork top. The cold liquid chilled her fingers, and she shivered as she brought it to her lips. Whispering before she drank, she said, "I accept my witch."

She gulped down the magical contents in one large swallow. It felt like ice to her throat, seizing her head like the worst ice cream headache she'd ever experienced. The cold kept her from tasting the combination of bitter herbs. When she could manage to gasp a breath through her frozen mouth, she coughed lightly. Jackson took the vial from her fingers and rolled it toward her camera bag.

"Anna?" He rubbed his hand along her back.

She nodded, unable to speak. Freezing cold turned to warmth, which turned to fire. Magic exploded from her limbs, pouring out of her like a painful waterfall. It spread out over the room, filling it with sparkling light.

"*To the victor a prize never to go.*" Anna's lips moved, but the voice was from the past. She looked up to see a ghosted image of herself, moving as she had that night.

"You break my heart, miss." Herbert's image appeared as large as he was in life. The photograph no longer mattered as it projected its secrets into life-sized holographic images like a play to be watched.

Jackson stood. Anna reached for his hand so he could help her to her feet. The sound of horse hooves filled the room, cutting off some of the past voices as more images appeared. Cynthia London stood at the door with her friends. The Sacred Order of Hairy Old Men held their ghostly masks, smiling and laughing as if they had no care in the world. They did not see her on the floor. The holographic image of Jackson moved past her, unhampered by the circle of protection. She shivered as the past Jackson brushed by her arm.

"Anna?" The present Jackson grabbed her hand and pulled her closer to him. "What is this? These people are alive. How can their ghosts be here? Did you summon their spirits?"

"You can have him, sweetheart!" Cynthia London's cry interrupted.

"I think it's a recording from the past." Anna looked at the red camera bag. It sat close to where she had placed it the night of the banquet. Ghostly images kept walking around, the low murmur of their voices exactly as they had been.

Herbert's hologram growled as he chased his wife into the main banquet hall with his pretend claws. Her attention turned to where Jackson had spoken to her. The words were harder to hear from where they were standing. She saw the tired, distrusting expression on her face as she'd answered him.

"I must have come off so rude," Anna observed. "I'm sorry. I was so nervous. I tried so hard not to stare at you."

"I thought you were beautiful," Jackson answered. "My heart was pounding so hard I kept telling myself to play it cool."

"I couldn't tell." Anna watched their past interactions a moment longer before turning her attention to where George would be.

Anna found George talking to Darla. The woman flirted, batting her eyelashes and touching his arms and chest a little too much. She smoothed down his tuxedo jacket and pretended to pet his werewolf half-mask like a pet. He brushed off Darla's hand as he looked to where Anna had been standing. His expression brightened as he made his way across the front hall. Darla's mouth opened in outrage at George's blatant dismissal, but she quickly hid the expression under an overly practiced smile.

It was hard to see her friend smiling and laughing, knowing what was to come. Anna glanced down and began to step over the candles.

Jackson placed a hand on her arm and stopped her. "You said we had to stay in the circle for protection."

"These aren't ghosts. They're memories. Besides, we have to leave the circle. It's the only way we can see and hear everything." Anna took a deep breath and held it as she stepped over the candles. Despite what she said, leaving the protective circle made her nervous. She glanced around to make sure none of the holographic images changed. They continued on with their play, completely unaware that Anna and Jackson were watching them. Her past self had packed up the antique camera.

Jackson joined her and placed a protective hand on her arm. The gesture was sweet, but she wasn't sure which one of them would be doing the protecting if magical elements decided to attack.

"...*this glorified poker club*," Anna's voice said as they neared her image. She looked around the room, seeing if anyone was watching George. There was only Darla, clearly upset that her date was talking to another woman.

"*Little does Tom know I'm holding out for a new boat*," George had said.

Anna walked away from her past conversation to watch Darla. The woman didn't hide her jealousy as she stared at George's back. Anna stepped through a moving holograph, not bothering to dodge the man as she continued to study the tall blonde's face. Anna hadn't been able to see it the night of the banquet, but now she watched Darla's lips moving ever so slightly. Anna leaned close to Darla's mouth and heard the whisper, *"How dare you? How dare you? You didn't change. I knew it."*

The words were strange for a woman who had only known George for seven hours. Then for her to show up at Ginger's house after his death? Anna frowned. This seemed more than just the typical possessiveness women developed when confronted with George's natural charisma.

She glanced back to see Jackson still stood by her old conversation. He probably hadn't heard it that night. Anna's ghost image handed George muffins. Part of her wanted to press pause, to stop what was coming.

"We need the truth," she whispered to herself, resisting the urge to stop.

Jackson went toward the banquet hall door. Even though the murmur of voices came through clearly, the ghosts seemed to fade and disappear when they moved into the banquet room. He stepped in, glanced around, and then turned to her shaking his head to indicate there was nothing to see.

"Who was that?" Darla asked, stroking her hand over George's chest with a pout.

"*Anna? She's one of my best friends,*" George answered. "*We've known each other a long time.*"

"*I thought I was your friend.*" Darla pushed out her bottom lip.

"*You're my date. My incredibly,*" George paused to kiss her pouty lips, "*sexy,*" he kissed her again, "*hot,*" he kissed her another time, "*date.*"

Darla giggled.

"*Wait here, Sandra. I'll be right back to continue this conversation.*" George tapped the tip of her nose and whistled softly as he strode toward the restroom.

Darla's widened eyes followed him. She began digging in her purse and pulled out a compact to check her makeup.

Anna was torn what to do, but in the end, she followed George and found him washing his hands. She leaned over to see if anyone else was in the stalls. They were empty.

Jackson joined her. They watched George fuss with his appearance before pulling out his phone. He pressed the video camera button and started recording as he tried to check the back of his head with it. He probably wanted to make sure his hair looked good from all angles.

"*Darla,*" Darla stated in a firm voice as she strode into the restroom. She latched the door lock.

"*What?*" George stopped his efforts to check the back of his head.

"*My name is Darla. You called me Sandra.*" Darla

placed her purse on the restroom counter with a hard thud. It was hard to tell if she was angry or merely playing at it.

"*Oh, sounds like I was a bad boy.*" George apparently thought Darla was playing around.

"*You forget women a lot, don't you?*" Darla continued.

George nodded. "*Yeah, I should be taught a lesson.*"

"*I couldn't agree more.*" Darla smiled and seductively walked toward him. She pursed her lips and leaned forward. "*I'm going to make sure you never forget me.*"

"George, no," Anna whispered as if the ghost could hear her plea.

George kissed Darla. He wrapped his arms around her waist, holding her tight, still clutching his phone. Her hand ran through his hair mussing the golden locks. When George jerked, trying to pull back, she held him tighter. They stumbled as he tried to get free and one of his shoes flew off, skidding across the floor.

Anna grabbed Jackson's arm. Her breathing deepened.

Jackson instantly pulled her against his chest. "You don't have to watch this."

Anna didn't turn away. She had to know the truth, wherever it led.

Darla let go of George with a loud gasp as if she'd been holding her breath with the force of the kiss. George fell backward. His phone skidded past Anna to go under a stall. It banged against a wall.

Darla watched George writhe on the tile floor. She leaned over, and pulled at his jacket, opening it, before jerking his fine dress shirt apart to bare his chest. Buttons flew all around. She flipped her fingers into his hair, making it look like they'd been in the throes of lovemaking.

She picked up the werewolf mask from by the sink and held it up. "*I gave you a chance to remember me. I came to this stupid party. And what did you do? You called me Sandra!*" She threw the mask on the floor in a fit of rage.

George tried to answer, but he convulsed and gasped. A rash spread from his mouth to his chin.

Darla touched up her lipstick in the mirror and smacked her lips a few times. She held up the makeup tube and looked at him through the mirror. "*Laced with pure silver. Makes it glittery, right?*"

George couldn't speak. Anna hated feeling so helpless. She started to reach for him, but Darla kept talking.

"*You know, I thought it was bizarre when the father of my child sent me a form letter with an odd list of dos-and-don'ts the day after my son was born, along with a check. You didn't even bother to show up. You just requested I didn't name him George and gave me a list of possible allergies to watch out for, especially silver. The paragraph you dedicated to it made me think maybe this was a hereditary allergy.*" Darla turned to face him. *"I thought we had an amazing time that week we met. I thought you liked me. But, then, fast forward three years, and I find a private investigator following me around taking pictures of me at the clubs, and on dates. It took all of two shots of whiskey to get him to spill all. You have the nerve to question my parenting?"* She laughed, though the sound held no humor. *"But I thought, 'No, Darla, give him a chance. Maybe he wants you to be a family. Maybe he's going to be a dad to Chester. Maybe he's going to step up to the plate and do the right thing.' You didn't even recognize me. You walked right up to me and used the same tired pick up line from three years ago. So, I thought, 'Hey, Darla, you're blonde now and more mature. Maybe he needs a chance.' Then what happens? You call me Sandra."*

George reached toward the door as if trying to escape.

"I bet you won't forget my name now." Darla took a deep breath, checked her reflection, and then began to scream as she unlocked the restroom door. The past rushed in to save George. The loud screams continued. Anna looked at Jackson, shaking her head as she trembled.

"Give them room. Back away," Herbert ordered.

Anna turned away from the scene. "I can't believe it. Darla did it. She killed George. We have to do something. We have to…"

"Call the sheriff," Dr. Magnus ordered.

Anna glanced at the holographic doctor.

"We need proof," Jackson said. "We can't just

call Detective August and say we know Darla is guilty of this case your lazy butt refused to open an investigation on."

"The phone. George was recording when Darla walked in. Maybe it caught the conversation?" Anna pushed open the toilet stalls. In the last one, she saw a phone jammed into a darkened corner. She picked it up. Her breathing deepened.

"George? No, George!" Ginger's scream echoed as all the figures disappeared.

Anna looked over the phone as they left the restroom. "It needs to be charged."

"Can you use your magic?" Jackson asked.

"Maybe?" Anna concentrated on the phone. It turned on.

Jackson chose the camera icon with a finger, and he was able to start playing the video. They watched in stunned silence. Not everything could be seen, but the words were clear enough to be unmistakable.

"We have it, Jackson," she whispered, torn between misery and relief. "Proof."

Chapter Twenty-Two

Jackson didn't leave Anna's side as they sat in the police station watching August as he viewed the camera footage for the second time. The detective's demeanor was stiff as he said, "It's as I suspected. I'm not pleased that you amateur sleuths took it upon yourself to do police work, and you're lucky I'm not arresting you for interfering in my official investigation, but I'm going to let it slide this time."

Jackson wanted to say so much to that little diatribe, but he held his tongue. There would be no changing blowhards like Detective August. He'd take this evidence and turn it into a win. He'd get his picture in the paper and pat himself on the back for all his hard work on a difficult case.

"We'll find this Sandra," August said. "If she is in town, we'll get her."

"Her name is Darla," Anna inserted. "She was

in town earlier today. I'm sure she hasn't left. I believe she was staying at one of the bed-and-breakfasts in town. Also, her son Chester should go to his grandmother, Ginger Madison. That is what George would have wanted."

August gave an expression that said he didn't see why he should care about the kid.

"Cop solves a murder, saves toddler and reunites him with his loving grandmother," Jackson stated loudly to Anna. "Now that's a story my editor would make sure went viral. That man would be a national hero. I bet major news stations would want to interview him. I bet—"

"Of course, all that will happen. I don't have the final say, but I'll be sure to put in a good word to the right people. The child should be with his grandmother," August broke in. He leaned over and jotted down a phone number on the back of his business card and handed it to Jackson. "This is my personal number. Call me, and we'll schedule an interview."

Anna nodded at Jackson grateful as August placed the phone in an evidence bag and took it toward a back room. "Thank you for that. Ginger will take care of the boy."

"I'll admit, writing a story about how that incompetent jerk saved the day will be hard, but at least the truth will be known. That's what really matters. We'll make sure Darla doesn't get away with it."

"I just hope he doesn't lose the evidence." Anna looked as if she might chase after August.

Jackson patted his jacket pocket where he kept his phone. "Don't worry about it. I sent myself a copy before we came inside the station. The truth will be known, one way or another."

"Judy," August said. "Call Ginger Madison and get her in here. I have some good news about my investigation into her son's murder."

"Ginger Madison? I thought you ruled that an accidental death due to an allergic reaction," Judy questioned, not moving away from her self-manicure to do as August told her.

"That was the official ruling of the doctor," August corrected. "But I didn't believe for a second that was the case. I knew in my gut that there was something more, and I was right. It was murder, and I solved it all by myself."

"Wow," Anna mumbled. "Can we get out of here? I can't watch that man's ego any longer."

Jackson nodded and escorted her outside. "Are you all right? I imagine you have to be going through a lot of emotions."

"I'm sad that this happened, relieved that the mystery is solved and justice will prevail, and I'm..."

"Anna, I love you," Jackson blurted. He hadn't

meant to say it, not here, not like this, but the words just tumbled out.

"I, ah...?" She blinked in surprise. An SUV pulled up to the station. The headlights shone brightly on them for a few seconds, causing them to turn their attention to the vehicle. It read, "SHER-IFF," along the side.

A uniformed law enforcement officer exited and lifted his hand. "Hey, Anna."

"Hey, Deputy March," Anna greeted.

The man had a large cowboy hat with a star-shaped badge. Black curls poked out his hat, looking a little longer than regulation cut—not that Jackson thought there were many regulations when it came to Sheriff Bull and her calendar cops. Next year's Everlasting law enforcement calendars had been popping up for sale everywhere in town.

"How's the coffee business?" March asked.

"Busy as ever," Anna said. "I have some new scones on the menu. There are some free ones with your name on it if you and the others stop by."

"Will do." March grinned. He touched the brim of his hat and walked inside the station.

"I'm sorry to interrupt your talk of muffins, but I just said I love you." Jackson refused to hold in his feelings any longer. "And you know what, I don't think it's because of a spell. Even if it was, I don't care. I love you, Anna Crawford. I love you."

"Scones," she whispered.

"What?" Jackson frowned.

"We were talking about scones," Anna corrected, her expression stunned. "You love me? You're sure that's what you meant to say? Because I used a lot of…" She glanced around and lowered her voice as if she were about to use a dirty word, "*magic* tonight when we were at the lodge. I'm not sure if that would cause side effects."

"Ok, seriously woman," Jackson declared, "I know you're a witch and if this feeling is a magical byproduct, then it's a part of you, and I love you more for it. I am under your spell, Anna, truly and completely. I love you. I lo—"

Anna's mouth pressed to his, and she kissed him. A strange thing happened as their lips met. Magical sensations flowed from her body into his as if a dam had broken loose. At that moment, there was no mistaking how she felt about him. She loved him as deeply as he had come to love her. It was fate as if the stars had held the story of their union close and waited for it to play out.

Jackson didn't know what the future would hold, but he knew he had finally found his home. Here. In Everlasting. With Anna. Forever.

Chapter Twenty-Three

"I knew it," Polly announced, as she came waddling down from the apartment Anna now shared with Jackson into the nearly empty coffee shop. She wore what could have only been described as a pink hazmat suit with yellow polka dot trim. The helmet flopped along her back. Her aunt held a photograph in her hand and waved it in front of Anna. "I knew he could see me. He's playing hard to get, but I got him!"

Anna looked up from the receipts to Polly. "Did you put away the chemicals in my darkroom like I asked you to when you were done with them? And you remembered to turn on the ventilation, right? You can't breathe those fumes."

"I know. You said it was dangerous, so I took precautions." Polly gestured to her outfit. "See."

Anna tried not to laugh at the overkill. All she

said was to turn on the exhaust fan and make sure she wore gloves.

Anna's attention turned to the few locals gracing the tables. They chuckled as they watched her aunt twirl around to show Anna her bio hazard protection. After a month of nonstop running around, Anna thought it was nice to have a small afternoon lull to get caught up on October's bookkeeping. The loss of tourist income would be noticeable, but she'd had a great month and couldn't complain. This year's Cranberry Festival had been one of the most profitable yet. From the looks of things, she'd be able to give Marcy a nice bonus for all the extra effort she ended up putting in. Anna even considered promoting the woman to the position of manager.

"By the way, Polly, Jolene called for you. The Cadillac is ready," Anna said. "She also wanted me to tell you she did not take out your front seat and put in a tank for Herman. She refuses to tear apart a classic for a crustacean."

"Are you listening to me? See for yourself." Her aunt stopped twirling and handed the photo to Anna. "I knew it."

Anna was almost scared to look. Polly had been begging her to use the camera to help her realize one of her deepest desires. Saying "yes" did go against Anna's better judgment, but a promise was a promise. She had made her aunt swear to stay out of the kitchen for the rest of the tourist season, and in return, she would let Polly take one picture with the camera before Anna packed it up and made it a display item in her shop, safely locked behind a glass case away from customers' hands.

It turned out, while Anna was playing amateur sleuth with Jackson, Marcy had been leaning on Polly for help. Anna couldn't be mad. Apparently, they'd made a lot of money on delivery orders. And, while Marcy was running all over town to make that happen, Polly had been holding down the fort. Which meant the mischievous witch had access to the ovens. Which further meant Polly was able to spread her ever-loving chaos all over the Cranberry Festival.

So far, the reports of Polly's magical mischief in the past month were limited to a few minor infractions. Hugh Lupine apparently went from cussing like a sailor on shore leave to uttering such delightfully entertaining curses as, "*you son-of-a-biscuit-bacon-loving-daisy-head*," and, "*I'm gonna shove my sunflower up your whoops a daisy*." Then there was Jerry, an elderly man who came in for blueberry muffins a couple of times a week. He managed to grow hair for the first time in two decades. Sadly, all fifteen of those hairs were different colors, and he looked like he had the world's worst rainbow comb over. To be fair, he was really proud of that comb over though.

Anna finally held up the photo to look at it. She

felt Jackson's presence behind her and knew he was projecting his consciousness to look over her shoulder without actually leaving the kitchen where he was supposed to be taking inventory. After she had accepted her witch heritage, Anna was able to sense when his spirit was walking around.

"Well?" Polly demanded.

The picture was taken from the inside of someone's kitchen. The lighting was bad, but Anna could just make out the shape of a cabinet door. "Is that…?"

"Cornelius," her aunt stated proudly, though it was hard to make out the face of the shadowy figure. "See, he's looking right at me. I knew it."

"Is he huddling in the corner? He looks terrified," Anna teased.

"No, he's standing, and…" Polly snatched the photo away. "Say what you want. He can see me. That's all I needed to know."

"Poor Captain Petey." Anna looked back at the receipts. "He's going to be so heartbroken."

"What do you mean? Petey and I have been friends for years. He knows I've been out ghost hunting. It's not fair that every other woman in town gets to see our local legend except me," Polly said. "By the way, I like the new hire. He has a good aura."

Her aunt's steps had a bounce to them as she ambled her way into Polly's Perfectly Magical

Mystical Wondrous World of Wonders with her photo. Jackson stopped his spirit walk, and she felt him leaving.

Anna glanced up to where Templeton bussed tables. He wore bright yellow pants and an orange shirt. When she asked about the new clothing preference, he explained that someone had almost run him over and he needed to make sure he could be clearly seen. It turned out that someone had been three-year-old Chester "George Jr." Madison on his tricycle. After Darla's arrest and subsequent plea of guilty in exchange for a twenty-five-year sentence, Ginger had managed to not only adopt Chester (who's middle name she changed to George Jr.) but was in the process of getting three of her other grandchildren—twins Aidan and Cadence, and a baby girl named Francis.

Seeing her attention, Templeton nodded and came to the counter. He glanced around and then laid a napkin on top of Anna's stack of receipts. Whispering, he said, "That thing I promised."

"Thank you," she answered just as quietly. "I'll keep it safe."

He gave a solemn nod and went back to work.

"What did he give you?" Jackson came up behind her and wrapped his arms around her waist. He kissed her neck. She sighed, instantly leaning back into him.

"That's between us." Anna laughed. "Hey, did I

tell you Templeton's mom called me? She's very grateful. She said that now he has some place to go and a job to do, he's much calmer. I think all he was looking for was a purpose to his day."

"It was very kind of you to help him," Jackson agreed.

"I think maybe I should get him a uniform of some sort," Anna mused, as she eyed the painful-to-look-at colors. "I think he'd enjoy it. What do you think?"

"Pirate? Dragon? Giant coffee bean?" Jackson chuckled. "Or do we just let him paint himself cranberry every year for the festival?"

"I was thinking more of an apron and a name tag with a special title on it." She snatched the napkin Templeton had given her away from Jackson when he tried to grab it.

"Tell me, what is it?" Jackson pleaded. "I'm dying to know."

"Fine." Anna held up the napkin with a collection of squiggles and dots on it. "It's a map to his home planet."

"I'm not sure I like other men giving you their address," Jackson teased. He lifted her hand and began kissing each knuckle as she resumed organizing her tax receipts. "Should I go have a talk with him and let him know you're my woman?"

"I don't know," she teased. "If you don't behave yourself, Mr. Argent, it looks like I do have other options out there in the universe." She paused and grabbed another receipt. "Do we have enough flour to finish off this week's orders? I'm so happy to be done with cranberries, I thought I'd try making peach scones with a little vanilla and heavy cream."

"I'm sorry, back to this Templeton thing. As beautiful as your green alien children would be, I'm not stepping aside for him." Jackson let go of her hand, and she reached for the calculator to total up a few of the remaining numbers. She laughed at his teasing. "He'll have to find his own Earthling."

Anna gasped. A white gold and diamond ring now graced her finger. The square cut stone was one of the most beautiful things she'd ever seen. Her hand shook as she stared at it, almost too afraid to move in case it disappeared. She hadn't felt him slip it on her finger.

"Anna Crawford, you have completely bewitched me," Jackson whispered into her ear. "I love you, and I don't ever want to let you go. Will you marry me?"

Anna opened her mouth, but no words came out. They had just moved in together, so he didn't have to pay for a hotel room while he stayed in town longer than he'd originally intended. With the festival over, the news outlet he worked for wasn't going to continue to foot the hotel bill. She hadn't thought he'd ask her to marry him, at least not anytime soon.

"Scones," she whispered.

"What?" Jackson turned her around to look at him.

"I was talking about scones," Anna said, too stunned to form her thoughts fully. "You want to marry me? You're sure that's what you meant to say? Because you only moved in three days ago…"

"Are you going to say scones every time I tell you something important?" he questioned.

"Yes." She nodded. "Yes, I love you, too. Of course, I'll marry you, Jackson!"

She threw her arms around him. At her enthusiastic response, locals started cheering. Polly came running out of her magic shop. "What'd I miss? Templeton, what's happening?"

"Meep," Templeton answered.

"A wedding?" her aunt clapped her hands as if understanding the strange man. "Marvelous! I'm going to call your third cousin four times removed and let her know the good news."

Cousin? Anna blinked in surprise, before dismissing the comment. Polly was probably making up family genealogy again.

Jackson twirled her around in his arms, and shouted, "Whoo-hoo, she said yes!"

When he set her down, Anna held him tight. "Jackson, I have to ask, are you sure? You won't regret settling down in Everlasting? It's not exactly the hotbed of activity you're used to as a journalist. I don't want you to get bored with small town life."

"I think there is plenty of mystery in Everlasting to keep me busy," he said. "And I always wanted to write a longer novel. Are you about done with those receipts? I want to take my fiancée out on the town to celebrate."

Anna lifted her stack of receipts and dropped them into a tax box. "All done." She grinned. "All in all, Mr. Argent, I would say this was a very successful festival."

"I'd say so, definitely." Jackson slipped his arms around her, pulling her to him. "It brought us together."

"I thought the mystery of George's twenty-three baby mamas brought us together," Anna corrected as she returned his embrace. She lifted her arms to wrap around his neck.

"I thought it was Aunt Polly's spell-casting that brought us together," Jackson said, leaning his mouth closer.

"Yeah, maybe that was it," Anna whispered. She grinned, unable to help herself as she added, "We fooled around with magic and spelled in love."

"Clever." His laugh was cut off as he kissed her. Some of the locals made, "*oooh*," and, "*ahhh*," noises.

Anna didn't care. Let them see her happiness. Pleasure and contentment bubbled up inside her.

She knew this is what she wanted. Jackson was her forever.

THE END

Want more cozy mysteries from Michelle M. Pillow?

Be sure to watch for books from Michelle M. Pillow! Sign up for her newsletter today so you don't miss out on a brand new series (Un)Lucky Valley! MichellePillow.com

Want to read how Marcy is cursed in love?

Check out:

Curses and Cupcakes

by Michelle M. Pillow

(Un)Lucky Valley Series

Better Haunts and Garden Gnomes

Any Witch Way But Goode

More Books Coming Soon

Magick, Mischief, & Kilts!

If you enjoyed this book by Michelle M. Pillow,
check out the magically mischievous, modern-day
Scottish, paranormal romance series:

Warlocks MacGregor®
Love Potions
Spellbound
Stirring Up Trouble
Cauldrons and Confession
Spirits and Spells
Kisses and Curses
More Coming Soon

MichellePillow.com

Newsletter

To stay informed about when a new book in the series installments is released, sign up for updates:

Sign up for Michelle's Newsletter
michellepillow.com/author-updates

About Michelle M. Pillow

***New York Times* & *USA TODAY*
Bestselling Author**

Michelle loves to travel and try new things, whether it's a paranormal investigation of an old Vaudeville Theatre or climbing Mayan temples in Belize. She believes life is an adventure fueled by copious amounts of coffee.

Newly relocated to the American South, Michelle is involved in various film and documentary projects with her talented director husband. She is mom to a fantastic artist. And she's managed by a dog and cat who make sure she's meeting her deadlines.

For the most part she can be found wearing pajama pants and working in her office. There may or may not be dancing. It's all part of the creative process.

Come say hello! Michelle loves talking with readers on social media!

www.MichellePillow.com

facebook.com/AuthorMichellePillow

twitter.com/michellepillow

instagram.com/michellempillow

bookbub.com/authors/michelle-m-pillow

goodreads.com/Michelle_Pillow

amazon.com/author/michellepillow

youtube.com/michellepillow

pinterest.com/michellepillow

Featured Titles from Michelle M.
Pillow

Magical Scottish Contemporary Romances

Warlocks MacGregor
Love Potions
Spellbound
Stirring Up Trouble
Cauldrons and Confession
Spirits and Spells

More Coming Soon

Paranormal Shapeshifter Romances

Dragon Lords Series

Barbarian Prince

Perfect Prince

Dark Prince

Warrior Prince

His Highness The Duke

The Stubborn Lord

The Reluctant Lord

The Impatient Lord

The Dragon's Queen

Lords of the Var® Series

The Savage King

The Playful Prince

The Bound Prince

The Rogue Prince

The Pirate Prince

Captured by a Dragon-Shifter Series

Determined Prince

Rebellious Prince

Stranded with the Cajun

Hunted by the Dragon

Mischievous Prince

Headstrong Prince

Futuristic Space Pirate Romance

Space Lords Series
His Frost Maiden
His Fire Maiden
His Metal Maiden
His Earth Maiden
His Woodland Maiden

To learn more about the Qurilixen World series of books and to stay up to date on the latest book list visit www.MichellePillow.com

Better Haunts and Garden Gnomes

NEED MORE AUNT POLLY?

Welcome to Lucky Valley
where nothing is quite what it seems.

Lily Goode wasn't aware she had an inheritance waiting for her in the form of a huge Victorian house in Lucky Valley, Colorado. Life might finally be coming together for her. That is if you don't count the endless home repairs, dealing with eccentric Aunt Polly who claims they're both witches, and Nolan Dawson the handsome home inspector who seems to have it out for her, then, sure, life is grand. Oh and not to mention the strange hallucinations and garden gnomes who are far more than lawn ornaments.

If mysterious accidents don't do her in, then the rebellious gnomes just might. With the help of Aunt Polly, it's up to Lily to discover who's sabotaging her new home and trying to drive the Goodes out of Lucky Valley once and for all.

From NY Times & USA TODAY Bestselling Author, Michelle M. Pillow, a Cozy Mystery Paranormal Romantic Comedy.

More Everlasting...

COZY PARANORMAL MYSTERY ROMANCE NOVELS

The Happily Everlasting Series

Dead Man Talking
by Jana DeLeon

Once Hunted, Twice Shy
by Mandy M. Roth

Fooled Around and Spelled in Love
by Michelle M. Pillow

Witchful Thinking
by Kristen Painter

Total Eclipse of The Hunt

by Mandy M. Roth

Curses and Cupcakes

by Michelle M. Pillow

An Everlasting Christmas

by Mandy M. Roth

Visit Everlasting

welcometoeverlasting.com

Dead Man Talking

by Jana DeLeon

Welcome to Everlasting, Maine, where there's no such thing as normal.

Meteorologist Zoe Parker put Everlasting in her rearview mirror as soon as she had her college degree in hand. But when Sapphire, her eccentric great-aunt, takes a tumble down the stairs in her lighthouse home, Zoe returns to the tiny fishing hamlet to look after her. Zoe has barely crossed the county line when strange things start happening with the weather, and she discovers Sapphire's fall was no accident. Someone is searching the light-house but Sapphire has no idea what they're looking for. Determined to ensure her aunt's ongoing safety, Zoe promises to expose the intruders, even though it means staying in Everlasting and confronting the past she thought she'd put behind her.

Dane Stanton never expected to see Zoe standing in the middle of her aunt's living room, and was even more unprepared for the flood of emotion he experiences when coming face to face with his old flame. Zoe is just as independent and determined as he remembered, and Dane knows she won't rest until Sapphire can return to the lighthouse in peace, so he offers to help her sort things out.

Armed with old legends, Sapphire's ten cats, and a talking ghost, Zoe has to reconcile her feelings for Dane and embrace her destiny before it's too late.

Once Hunted, Twice Shy

by Mandy M. Roth

Welcome to Everlasting, Maine, where there's no such thing as normal.

Wolf shifter Hugh Lupine simply wants to make it through the month and win the bet he has with his best friend. He's not looking to date anyone, or to solve a murder, but when a breath taking beauty runs him over (literally) he's left no choice but to take notice of the quirky, sassy newcomer. She'd be perfect if it wasn't for the fact she's the grand-daughter of the local supernatural hunter. Even if he can set aside his feelings about her family, Pene-lope is his complete opposite in all ways.

Penelope Messing wanted to get away from the harsh reminder that her boyfriend of two years dumped her. Several pints of ice cream and one plane ticket to Maine later, she's ready to forget her troubles. At least for a bit. When she arrives in the sleepy little fishing town of Everlasting, for a surprise visit with her grandfather, she soon learns that outrunning one problem can lead to a whole mess of others. She finds herself the prime suspect in a double homicide. She doesn't even kill spiders, let alone people, but local law enforcement has their eyes on her.

The secrets of Everlasting come to light and Penelope has to not only accept that things that go bump in the night are real, but apparently, she's destined for a man who sprouts fur and has a bizarre obsession with fish sticks. Can they clear Penelope's name and set aside their differences to find true love?

Curses and Cupcakes

by Michelle M. Pillow

Welcome to Everlasting, Maine, where there's no such thing as normal.

Marcy Lewis is cursed (honestly and truly) which makes dating very interesting. With a string of loser boyfriends behind her, she's done looking for love in all the wrong places. That is until the new firefighter arrives in the sleepy seaside town of Everlasting. Nicholas Logan is unlike any other man she's ever had in her life. When someone starts sending her photographs that raise a red flag it soon becomes apparent that she's not just cursed, she's in serious danger.

Nicholas doesn't know what to make of the charismatic young woman managing the local coffee shop. As a string of mysterious fires begin popping up around town, the two unite in search of clues as to who or what is responsible, discovering along the way that things are very rarely what they seem to be.

Witchful Thinking

by Kristen Painter

Welcome to Everlasting, Maine, where there's no such thing as normal.

Charlotte Fenchurch knows that, which is why she's not that surprised when a very special book of magic falls into her hands at the library where she works. As a fledgling witch, owning her own grimoire is a dream come true. But there's something...mysterious about the book she just can't figure out.

Leopard shifter Walker Black knows what's odd about the book. It's full of black magic and so dangerous that it could destroy the world. Good thing the Fraternal Order of Light has sent him to Everlasting to recover it and put it into safe storage.

If he has to, he'll even take the witch who owns it into custody.

That is until he meets Charlotte and realizes she's not out to watch the world burn. She's sweet and kind and wonderful. Suddenly protecting her is all he wants to do. Well, that and kiss her some more. But dark forces seem determined to get their hands on the book, making Charlotte their target, and Walker worries that he won't be able to protect her from them – or the organization he works for.

Can Walker and Charlotte survive the onslaught of danger? Or is that just witchful thinking?

Visit Everlasting
https://welcometoeverlasting.com/

Please Leave a Review

Please take a moment to share your thoughts by reviewing this book. Thank you for reading!

Be sure to check out Michelle's other titles at www.michellepillow.com

Made in the USA
Monee, IL
08 February 2020